A Woman In Red

Randolph Cooper

Published by Trellis Publishing, 2021.

A WOMAN IN RED

First edition. July 8, 2021.

Copyright © 2021 Randolph Cooper.

ISBN: 979-8224938261

Written by Randolph Cooper.

A WOMAN IN RED

RANDOLPH COOPER

Chapter 1

"You failed."

She looked confused, she just looked at him without saying anything for a while before he said, "I've purged you from my system."

She twisted her red hair and smiled at the withering shell of a man lying in the hospital bed. She glanced back to make sure no one was listening before saying, "I'm surprised, I won't lie. Of course, I don't really need you anymore. You no longer have anything to offer me."

"Wrong, you can say that, but we both know you failed."

"You'll be dead soon. I'd call that success. Did you think I just wanted your money? Do you think I didn't know you snuck off to talk to your lawyer?"

The man in the hospital bed did not reply. He thought his clandestine visits had gone undetected.

"You really thought you fooled me?" she said with a smile, "If I thought it would have mattered I would have stopped you. I'm your wife. I get it all regardless."

"No, you don't. When it comes to being a traitorous bitch you are certainly first class, but when comes to fucking someone over legally? You're out of your league. How do you think I got that fortune? As of yesterday, we are no longer man and wife."

"Impossible. I didn't sign anything."

"You didn't have to. I may have been smitten with you but my lawyer, god bless his cold heartless soul, wasn't. You signed a prenup giving me the right to end the marriage on my own without your input for the first year. I slipped in just under the deadline."

"Why?"

"Because it was the only thing I could do to you."

"I was still your wife. This is still a community property state."

"Sure, but you should have read the fine print. You're only entitled to assets acquired after our marriage."

"Your family disowned you long ago. You don't even have anyone to leave your money to."

It hurt to laugh, but he managed anyway. It was difficult to sit up but he managed that as well. He looked directly into her jade green eyes as he said, "They don't all hate me, but even if they did, they'll take my money."

She moved close and put her hand on his bare arm, "Why would you do this to me?"

"Save it. It's not going to work anymore. It doesn't work anymore. I know what you are."

"You are an old fool whose mind has gone along with his body."

"Speaking of old," he told her, "Since I've got wise I've noticed some more wrinkles on your pretty face."

She had noticed them too, but she didn't want to give him the satisfaction, "Along with everything else you're losing your eyesight."

"I see better than I have in almost a year."

"You've gone senile."

"Maybe, or maybe my lawyer wasn't the only one I was talking to behind your back."

She pulled her hand away and left him to die.

Chapter 2

"I can't believe you got this lucky," Chad said as Tim sat down at the table.

Hank, holding three pints of beer in his big hands said, "No shit. I can't think of anyone less deserving."

Tim shrugged and picked up one of the pints Hank set down. Even though Hank was kidding, Tim thought the gym teacher was right. Much like Chad, he had a hard time believing his recent good fortune himself.

"In fact," Hank said, "Why am I buying the drinks with Bill Gates Junior sitting here?"

"Because, it's your turn," Chad told him.

"I can get them," Tim said as reached for his wallet.

Hank held up his hand, "Dude, I'm kidding. We've been rotating who buys the first round for what? Five years? I don't care how much money any of us inherits this is the way we're doing it."

Tim nodded and took his hand off his wallet and picked up his beer. Thinking how it wasn't long ago he was a lonely fourth-grade teacher. His salary was enough he wasn't struggling, but he was hardly thriving. He had a place to live and a car that worked, he could eat out once in a while, but the savings account wasn't growing very fast. His love life wasn't working out very well either since Jennifer, a fellow elementary school teacher, ended their relationship. Dates had become few and far between. The fact was, he still had a thing for Jennifer, or at least he did until Pamela came into his life.

Jennifer left him for an investment banker and Tim couldn't help but think his meager teacher salary, which wouldn't be changing all that much over the next decade had something to do with her dropping him. Tim, however, liked being a teacher. He felt he was smart enough to get into something more lucrative but knew he'd be miserable if he did.

It seemed a no-win situation. He could be lonely and never get rich, or he could leave the job he actually loved to spend forty to sixty hours a week doing something he did not love for more money and perhaps better prospects for his love life.

At one of his lowest points, friends like his fellow teacher and drinking buddy Chad told him he was being way too cynical. Chad had found himself a wife on the same teacher's salary as Tim. His other fellow teacher and drinking buddy Hank had a steady girlfriend. They told him there was someone out there for him. They told him he could have the job he loved and find a woman who loved him too.

He didn't believe them until he met Pamela. He ran into her at the same bar he, Chad, and Hank were drinking IPA's at. It was a little hole in the wall dive bar with a better than average beer selection close to their school that had become part of their end of the week ritual. They had been coming here on Friday's after school since Chad and Tim were hired and Hank, who had only been teaching a year longer, invited them out five years ago. There was a time when others, including Jennifer, which was how she and Tim hooked up, would join them, but mostly it was just the three of them.

When they first started it wasn't unusual to walk out of Phil's Tavern around closing time, but since Chad got married and Hank pretty much got married except in the legal sense they didn't stay as long. One beer, after school got out, then they could all be home for dinner.

Since Tim was just eating something microwaved with just his television for company, he often stayed behind and had another beer or four at the bar. Phil's Tavern was not the kind of place singles went to meet people. It was at best a neighborhood bar, though it's location in a dying mini-mall next to an industrial park tucked between a nail salon and a long-closed video store wasn't really in anyone's neighborhood.

The statuesque redhead who came in after Hank and Chad left immediately looked out of place. Tim wondered if she was lost. She looked like she should be somewhere modeling swimwear instead of ordering a beer from Phil.

He never considered talking to her. There was no question he was attracted to her, but it was clear looking at her that she could do much better than him. He was actually thinking about leaving when she sat down on the stool next to him.

"Do you mind if I join you? It looks like we've both been stood up," she asked.

Tim found her being stood up hard to believe on two levels, the first someone would stand her up and the second someone thought taking a woman like this to dive like Phil's was a good idea.

"Clearly the person who did this to you is an idiot," Tim told her, "You're better off without him."

She raised her glass saying, "You're right, and the foolish girl who failed to meet you is an idiot as well."

"Perhaps they deserved each other," Tim said as they clinked glasses. He decided if she wanted to think he wasn't the type of guy who would be spending Friday night alone in a dive bar on purpose he would let her.

"Perhaps we deserve each other," she told him.

He didn't think he deserved her but she felt different. He figured every time they went out for the next six months she would figure out she looked like a supermodel and he was an average looking fourth-grade teacher. Even after he proposed and she accepted he still found himself wondering when she would figure it out.

"You're awfully quiet tonight," Chad said to Tim, breaking Tim out of his trip down memory lane.

"He's probably thinking about how to spend all that money his Uncle left him when it clears," Hank said.

"That will be easy," Chad told them, "I'm guessing Pam will want a big wedding now that you guys can afford it. Hell, Penny and I had a big wedding and we really couldn't afford it. I'm still paying for it."

"If that's what she wants," Tim said as he thought about their wedding. It wasn't until after the ceremony in Las Vegas at one of the Chapels designed for quick nuptials he began to feel she was with him for the long haul. They chose Vegas because neither really had any family, Tim had only met the Uncle who was about to make him rich once or twice, so there was no reason for a big wedding.

"I don't see why you two even got married in the first place," Hank said, "All it does it cost money and create paperwork."

"Just be glad you have a girl who feels the same way," Chad said, "I tried that route with Penny but she wanted the ring."

"That's because she wanted those big teacher bucks you're making," Hank told him.

"She just got a promotion. If we get a divorce she'll be paying me alimony."

Tim shook his head as he said, "You know if my Uncle gave me all his money before I met Pam it would never have worked out."

"Why? Do you think she loves living off that teachers salary? If that's the case Penny and I will take your money. We're willing to make that sacrifice for the good of your marriage," Chad told him.

"I'm glad to see you're here for me, but we'll be fine. I was just thinking I would have never believed she liked me for me. Hell, I look at her and still have a hard time believing it. I would have assumed she just wanted the money."

"I can see why you would think that," Hank said, "but I bet you would have still married her."

Tim thought about that for a second before saying, "Yeah, I mean she would still be her, and I love her. It's just better this way, you know. It's nice knowing when the preacher said for richer or for poorer and she said 'I do' that she meant it."

"They actually say that part in Vegas? I figured they just said 'Do you two want to married yes or no?' and then if you both said yes they said kiss the bride and pay the clerk on the way out," Hank said.

"Pretty close, I think we paid extra for the full vows."

The dark bar filled with light for a second as the door opened and a man walked in. Phil's was rarely crowded and since it was still afternoon Phil, Chad, Hank, and Tim usually had the place to themselves. They had been coming here long enough they knew most of the other regulars. None of them had seen this man before.

The tall stranger with jet black hair stopped and looked at them. He stared long enough it was beginning to get uncomfortable before he took a seat at the bar. Even in the dimly lit room, Tim noticed the man's eyes were green. Normally this was the last thing he would notice on another man, but he had only seen eyes like this on one other person. His wife.

"What's the first thing you're going to buy when the check clears?" Hank asked as they went back to their beers and quit staring at the stranger.

"Other than a round of beers for you guys?" Tim said, "I have no idea."

"A car?" Chad asked.

"Maybe for Pam. I was talking to the lawyer and I'm pretty sure I'm going to get my Uncles old Ferrari as part of the inheritance."

"Awesome" Chad said.

Tim finished his beer and asked, "Do you guys want another round? I'm buying."

"Nah," Chad said, "I'm meeting the wife for dinner."

"Me too," Hank told him, "But I will want a ride in that Ferrari."

"So will I," Chad added.

"I think that can be arranged. I probably ought to be heading home myself," Tim said, thinking it was nice to have a reason to go home.

Tim was getting behind the wheel of his soon to be obsolete Honda Civic when he noticed the green-eyed man standing in front of his car. The man stared at him and Tim wondered if the guy was looking for trouble. Tim put his car into reverse thinking this stranger would have to find trouble elsewhere.

He looked up and saw the man holding up his hand, signaling for Tim to stop. Tim hesitated and the man walked to his window.

Tim lowered the window a few inches, giving himself some protection in case the stranger tried something but allowing him to hear what the man had to say before asking "Can I help you?"

"Tim Farrel?" the stranger asked.

"Yeah, how do you know me? Did I teach your kid?"

"You don't know me."

"How do you know my name?"

Instead of answering the stranger said, "You need to get away from her."

"Who?"

"Cassandra."

"I don't know a Cassandra."

"She lives in your apartment."

"I think you have the Tim Farrel, there's no Cassandra living in my apartment."

The stranger pointed to Tim's left hand, which was resting on the steering wheel and said, "You wear a wedding band."

Tim looked at the plain gold band on his finger and then back to the stranger and said, "Yeah, that's what married guys do. I've got to go."

"You married Cassandra."

"No, I married Pamela. Like I said, you've got the wrong Tim Farrel."

"No, it doesn't matter what she calls herself. It is Cassandra and she will be the end of you."

"Look," Tim said, "I don't know who the hell you are and I don't care..."

"You should care," the stranger interrupted, "I'm here to save your life."

"Thanks, but no thanks. I've got it under control. In fact, my life is better than ever right now."

"An illusion designed to lure you into her trap."

"Her trap?"

"Yes. My sister is very devious and deadly this way."

"Your sister?"

"Yes."

"Now I'm sure you have the wrong guy. My wife is an only child."

"Your wife is a predator, and you are her prey. She carries the venom like the desert rat spider, you must not let her infect you."

Tim shook his head. He had no doubts the person in front of him was either crazy and currently either off his meds or on some he should have avoided. He wished he never engaged in the first place. While it was too late for that there was no reason to let this odd stranger waste any more of his time.

"I'll keep that mind," Tim told him, "I have to go."

"Don't go back to her. Like the spider, she will seduce you and drain you of all you hold dear. It is what she does. She is incapable of doing anything else."

"Whatever," Tim said as he put the car back into reverse. Before he could pull away the stranger put his fingers through the crack in the window and held on. He didn't try to push the window open or break the glass, he just held the glass. Tim feared if he kept hanging on when he started to drive the stranger would be dragged by the car. Tim was certain the man was insane but he didn't want to hurt him.

"You need to let go," Tim told him.

The stranger leaned down so he was face to face with Tim. They were inches from each other, the stranger was close enough his breath fogged the glass between them.

"You need to listen to me," he said, "your uncle..."

"You need to let go of my window," Tim interrupted. He had lost patience with the crazy man's nonsense and did not want to hear another word.

They locked eyes, but Tim could only hold his gaze for a moment before he looked away.

"The venom is already in you," the stranger told him, "You need to get away, do not go back to her."

Tim felt the anger start to rise, until this moment he was more afraid than anything else. At this moment, however, he was thinking he could beat the crazy out of the stranger. The fact Tim was never much of a fighter didn't matter. He was reaching for the door handle when the stranger let go and took a step back.

Tim sensed it was the stranger who was now afraid instead of the other way around.

"You're not as strong as he was. Perhaps it is too late for you," the stranger told him.

"Stay the hell away from me or it will be too late for you too," Tim told him as backed out of the parking space and left the green-eyed stranger standing there.

Chapter 3

"I guess the weirdo was kind of right," Tim said as Pamela laid her head on his bare shoulder. He came home to find she cooked dinner, a stew of some kind Tim had never had before. The smell was almost intoxicating and he found he was starving. After dinner, she led him back to the bedroom.

As always, even after being with her for months, he was amazed a woman as attractive as Pamela wanted to be with him.

"The weirdo?" she asked.

"Yeah, this guy came up to my car as I was leaving Phil's. He started ranting all sorts of nonsense. Among the things he said was I'd be seduced and drained. I'd say you seduced me all right, and I'm certainly drained."

She moved so she was on top of him, sitting up so he could take in her naked body. He was thinking he might not be totally drained after all.

"That's funny, I thought it was you who seduced me," she said as she ran her hands over his chest.

He looked up into her jade eyes and maybe for the first time since meeting her the mood to ravish her faded. He couldn't help but think of the stranger who had the same eyes. Until he saw the man at the bar he had never seen anyone with Pamela's color. He looked away to her body and the mood came right back. He smiled at her saying, "He left out the part where you cooked me dinner. That was delicious by the way."

"Thank you," she said, "It's an old family recipe. Did this weirdo say anything else?"

"He mentioned his sister."

"His sister?"

"Someone named Cassandra," he told her. Hearing the name seemed to make her recoil like she touched something hot, but soon she was back to smiling at him as she rubbed her hands on his chest and rotated her hips against his crotch.

"What did he say about this Cassandra?" she asked.

"Not much other than her name."

"Are you sure?"

This seemed an odd question to Tim, but with her writhing against him, it was hard to think about why she asked him in what was an almost accusatory way.

"I'm pretty sure he just said the name," Tim replied, "He also talked about spiders and told me not to go home if you're wondering."

"I'm glad you didn't listen. I was really looking forward to draining you tonight," she said before leaning over and putting her lips to his.

She pulled back after a long kiss and he said, "I think he told me it was too late for me, whatever that means."

"It means you're mine," she said.

He ran his hands across her back as he said, "I'm fine with that."

"Of course you are," she told him before bringing her lips to his one more time.

They kissed and soon were making love for the third time since dinner. Afterward, she and Tim were both exhausted and fell asleep in each other's arms.

Chapter 4

Since he chose to spend yesterday afternoon hanging out with Hank and Chad and the night in bed with Pamela, Tim still had papers to grade on Saturday afternoon. He took a stack of essay's on Abraham Lincoln and the civil war into the spare bedroom and got to work.

Reading a bunch of nine-year-olds interpretation of Lincoln's leading of the Union could be tedious at times. They did their best, but there wasn't a lot of unique insight. It was day's like this, staying indoors on a perfectly nice spring Saturday afternoon when he thought he would quit teaching and live off the small fortuned his eccentric Uncle left him. He figured he would finish the year, it was getting close to being over anyway and then call it a career.

After powering through the papers he opened up his laptop and checked his email, hoping for news on the fortune due to be coming his way. There was nothing new in his inbox but junk. Since he had the internet up Tim typed in Desert Rat Spiders. He wasn't sure why, in fact as he typed he figured the stranger with his wife's eyes may have just made them up.

The internet said otherwise. It turned out they were a very large species of tarantula found only in high parts of the Saharan Desert. The name rat spider didn't come from the way they looked, they looked very much like any other tarantula, but because on occasion they would hunt and eat rodents.

While they were certainly big compared to other spiders they were still spiders, the idea of a spider eating a rat, even a malnourished one struggling to survive out on the unforgiving desert seemed far-fetched to Tim. According to the website, many scientists found this unlikely as well but over time it became accepted the tarantula did indeed take down the occasional rat. The secret Tim read was to a rat the tarantula's venom was like a mix of L.S.D. and Ecstasy. Basically, the rodent went into such a euphoric state after the initial bite it hardly noticed the spider was wrapping him in a cocoon of webbing in preparation for being a meal.

It took a long time for a spider, or even a family of spiders to eat a rat, days or even weeks. Apparently, desert rats taste best to tarantula's when they're still alive. The venom was apparently powerful enough the rat remained in a euphoric state even as spiders feasted on its insides.

There was a video to prove it. Tim wasn't sure he wanted to see a spider eat a rat but he clicked on it anyway. It was done with time-lapse photography so the week-long process of devouring a happy rat could be viewed in a couple of minutes.

Tim was never a big fan of rodents. He didn't even like gerbils and had no problems setting traps for mice if need be. He never thought he could feel bad for a rat, but watching this one getting eaten by a spider made him feel sympathetic to the vermin.

He closed the tab. His email was still up and he saw he had a new message. It was from someone named Annabelle Thompson and the subject was your Uncles ex-wife.

He opened the email. He knew his uncle had a wife and she was part of the reason he didn't have the money yet, but he had no contact with her. There was no reason to, his uncle's lawyer was in charge of dealing with her. He wondered if she were contacting him, perhaps angling to get some more of his uncles money.

He could understand why she might feel that way. He didn't know anything about her, but the lawyer told him she was much younger than he was and the marriage only lasted a year. Had the marriage lasted thirteen months she would have got it all instead of Tim.

He opened the email.

The first thing he saw was a list of names. Tim didn't recognize any of them, except at the bottom was his Uncles. Above him was the name, Annabelle. Tim noticed the names, there were eight in all, alternated between male and female.

He scrolled down and written at the bottom was: "Don't add your name to this list. Perhaps it is not too late."

Reading this last part made him think of the green-eyed stranger. He was trying to figure out how the stranger had gotten his email address when Pamela called to him from the other room.

"Are you almost done?" she asked.

He was done. If this email was from the stranger he didn't want anything to do with it. He deleted the email and closed the laptop before saying, "Just finished."

"Then come see me."

"It's a nice day. We should go do something outside," he said as he went to the door. He was feeling claustrophobic, something that happened to him when he spent too long in the apartment.

Tim went into the living room and saw her standing without a stitch of clothing except for a pair of high heel shoes on her feet.

"You look upset," she told him.

He didn't want to tell her he was sad about a long dead rat on the other side of the world so he said, "No, I'm just tired. Grading papers takes it out of me."

"Soon you won't have to grade another paper," she said as she walked to him.

"Yeah, that's true.

She went to him, wrapping her arms around him and pulling him close, once he was against her body she said, "I was thinking there was something we could do inside."

Tim felt her touch and no longer thought of the poor rat dying slowly but happily, or the list of names sent by the stranger, or any of his feelings of claustrophobia. All he could think about was Pamela. In her arms all he felt was euphoria.

Chapter 5

The next morning at school Tim didn't feel very well. If he had been drinking he would have thought he had a hangover, but he hadn't had anything to drink since his beer on Friday. His headache wasn't acute, but it was persistent, the Advil he swallowed with his morning coffee had no effect. Even though he got plenty of sleep the night before he was strangely tired, even though he had only been up a few hours. Breakfast wasn't sitting well in his stomach.

When lunch came around instead of eating in the teacher's lounge he stayed in his classroom just because the idea of walking down the hall sounded like torture in his current condition.

With no one to talk to he retrieved his laptop. Finding out he was officially a millionaire would make him feel better. Unfortunately, there was no official word in his inbox. He thought about the odd list of names which seemed to come from the weird stranger.

He deleted the message but even deleted messages could be retrieved within a certain time frame. He clicked the icon marked deleted messages and found the list of names. He put the first one into his computer's search engine.

Before he could look at the results he began to cough. The coughing was so violent he fell out of his chair. He gained control for a moment and then looked at his hands which were wet with the blood and mucus he had just coughed up.

Tim tried to stand but only go to one knee before he passed out.

Chapter 6

"How's he doing?" Chad asked.

Tim wanted to answer, he could hear just fine but when he tried to call to his friend from the bedroom all that came out was a croaking sound. He managed to get himself upright. He paused to gain the energy to walk into the other room.

He heard Pamela cry a little before she said, "I don't know. No one knows. I'm just glad they let him come home instead of staying in the hospital."

"Can we see him?" Tim heard Hank ask.

"Of course," Pamela said, "I'm sure he wants to see you guys."

"We were thinking we should take him to Phil's," Chad said, "Get him out of the apartment and give you a break. You've been with him non-stop all week."

"That doesn't seem like a good idea. He shouldn't drink."

"Of course, but it will make him feel better just getting out. We'll make sure he's okay," Hank said.

"It really won't be any different than when he came to school yesterday to talk to the kids," Chad added.

"That was different," Pamela said, "after they found him spasming on the floor covered in his own blood they needed to see him at least standing up. The bartender at Phil's doesn't need to see Tim to stop having nightmares."

"It will do him some good..."

"No," Pam interrupted, "I won't allow it."

Tim entered the room, fully dressed and said, "I think it's an excellent idea. We can take my Ferrari. I haven't even sat in it yet."

"You're in no condition to drive."

"I promised Chad he could drive it."

"Fine, but I'm coming along."

"You'll have to drive your own car. The Ferrari only seats two."

"Hank can drive me."

"Sorry," Hank said, "I've got to go straight home after."

"Fine, I'll take my car."

With that decided, Tim found the keys to the car he felt he would die before he got to drive and gave them to Chad. They went to the garage of the apartment building and got in the sports car, which looked odd among the pickup trucks and economy sedan most of the residents drove.

Once Tim was buckled in Chad said, "Hang on tight. We're going to have to lose her."

Chapter 7

The car chase never really materialized. Once Chad got them on the freeway Tim's Honda couldn't keep up. The Honda was nowhere in sight when Chad took an exit and headed out of town.

"Where are going?" Tim asked more than once, but Chad never said. After a while, Tim drifted off to sleep.

When he woke up he was in a bed looking at the wood ceiling of some sort of cabin. He looked over and saw Chad and Hank in chairs watching him. He tried to sit up but found he was tied down with leather straps.

"What the hell is going on?" he managed to ask.

"When I found you in your classroom your computer was still up. I could see what you were looking at," Hank told him.

"So?" Tim asked. The fact was he could hardly remember anything from that day.

"So, I finished the search. I searched all the names in the email. Then I sent a message back to whoever sent it."

"Was it the green-eyed stranger?" Tim asked.

"Yes," a new voice said.

Tim looked over to see the stranger standing in the doorway. He looked back to Hank and said, "This guy is crazy."

"Maybe but you should look at this," Hank said as he moved to a table in the corner of the room and brought back four sheets of paper. Each one had a picture of a woman.

"Do you recognize her?"

"Yeah," Tim said, "It looks like Pam only with brown hair."

Hank changed the picture.

"Pam with red hair," Tim said.

He showed her the last two.

"So my wife had changed her hair color?" Tim said, "Seems an odd reason to kidnap me."

"She changed her name too," Chad said, "the names on the list are all her."

"The names of the men are, or were, her husbands," Hank told him.

"What do mean were?" Tim asked.

"They all died, all of them became sick, a lot like you."

"Bullshit," Tim told them.

"I printed out the obits too," Chad said, "Do you want to read them?"

"Seeing how I don't have anything better to do why not."

Chad went to the table and handed Tim the stack of obits.

After reading the first one Tim said, "This one proves it's bullshit. It's ten years old. Pam would have been a teenager."

"How old did 'Pam' say she was?" the stranger asked.

Tim thought about it but couldn't come up with an answer. He went back to reading the obits. When he came to the last one he didn't have to read it. It was his Uncle, he had already read it.

"So, are you seriously saying Pam was married to my Uncle?"

"Yes," the stranger said, "He divorced her and sent his fortune to you. This made her angry, so she targeted you. You were an easy mark for someone like her."

"Except when we met I hadn't inherited a dime. I had no idea my Uncle was going to leave me anything."

"She knew," Hank said, "Did you know your Uncles first lawyer died of starvation and dehydration? In his home with a fully stocked refrigerator?"

"My sister didn't take her time with the lawyer," the stranger said, "While your Uncle was dying slowly she was meeting you at the bar."

"Did you notice how once the money became your's officially you suddenly got sick?" Chad said.

Tim shook his head, "I don't believe it."

"You don't want to believe it." the stranger said.

"How did she make me sick? And if she poisoned these four guys wouldn't someone notice?"

"It is not a toxin known to man," the stranger said.

"What does that mean?"

"It means my sister is not what you think she is."

"What is she?"

"A predator, like a spider. She feeds off humans and they keep her young."

"A spider who cares about money?"

"I said like a spider. She enjoys the spoils of being rich."

"Now I know you are all full of shit."

"It's true," Hank said.

"I wish it wasn't," Chad added, "but it is."

"You seriously believe this?"

They pointed at the stranger who was no longer a man and Tim believed it too.

"Wait," Tim said, "If your sister feeds off people what do you feed off of?"

"He doesn't drain them like his sister," Chad said, "He just takes enough to get by."

Tim looked over at the stranger still in his half bug form and asked, "Is that true?"

"No," he told them as his arachnid face twisted into a smile, "it's not true at all. My sister and I just have different ways of playing with our food."

Hank pulled the gun from under the bed and shot the green-eyed man spider six times. After the stranger fell he said, "I never believe that 'I take enough to get by' bullshit."

"What do we do now?" Tim asked.

"We find out if the part he told us about you getting better as long as you're away from Pam is true," Hank said as Chad went to check the body.

"Is it dead?" he asked.

"Yeah."

Hank held up the gun and said, "Then after you get better we go kill another bug."

YOU CAN'T HIDE FROM A VAMPIRE

VICTOR NEIL

Kristin came out of the office building and found herself greeting by her two partners in crime, Jade and Heather.

It would be another routine Friday night for the trio. A night out clubbing and dancing.

But lately they each had their own money woes, none worst that Kristin as she looked inside the wallet inside her purse.

Two dollars and a coupon for some McNuggets.

"I can't believe I spent all my money," Heather said.

"I believe it, with what little you make," Jade said.

"Excuse me?" Heather asked with incredulity. "Where do you work again? I believe it's called a pet shop.

"Both of those are better than being an office clerk," Kristin said.

"I'll trade you," Heather said.

"Let me ask my boss tomorrow."

The three young women walked through the parking lot toward Kristin's vehicle, the last remaining car in the lot.

"I had such a bright future until my stupid parents cut me off," Heather said.

"Maybe you shouldn't have banged that married man in their bed, Kristin said, laughing as she and Jade did a fist bump.

Heather did not look amused. "He was so hot."

"And so married," Jade said.

"His wife didn't get him."

"And neither did you. "

" Oh, I had him," Heather said, "And it was wonderful."

Kristin amusingly shook her head as she fished her keys out of her purse.

Jade hugged herself and shivered. "Hurry up. It's cold."

"Maybe you wouldn't be cold if you had worn more clothes," Heather said, pointing at Jade's get up of a halter top and mini-skirt.

"I wouldn't talk," Jade said.

Heather popped the door locks.

"I'll have the heater going in no time," Kristin said, getting in behind the wheel.

Heather opened the front passenger door for herself. Jade squeezed past and scooted over to the middle.

"What the hell?"

"I need body heat," Jade said.

"Who are you shitting? You just want your stash in the glove compartment."

"That, too."

Heather rolled her eyes and got in, the women now squished together in the front seat.

"What stash?" Kristin asked.

"Are you really that naive?"

Kristin gave Heather a smirk, then started the car and blasted the heater.

Jade reached over Heather to open the glove compartment and searched the contents, finding her baggie with a joint inside.

"Stop it!" Heather said, not enjoying Jade crowding her as she slammed the compartment closed.

Jade held up the baggie and smiled. "Come to momma."

The sight of the baggie alarmed Kristin. "You hid that in MY car?"

"I knew what you would say if I asked," Jade said, opening the baggie and taking out the joint.

"Oh, no you don't. Not in my car."

"Since when are you so uptight?"

"Since I got pulled over last week for speeding," Kristen took the baggie and sealed it back up. "You can wait until we get back to Kristin's place," Heather said.

"I don't want her smoking there, either."

"Deal with it," Heather said.

Kristin opened her mouth to argue but thought better of it. Jade reluctantly stuffed the baggie into her purse. Then she sniffed the air.

"What's that smell?" Jade asked.

Her friends also took a whiff and didn't care for the odor.

"Smells like old lady perfume," Heather said. "Hey Kristin, did you-"

A woman suddenly popped up in the backseat, looking to be in pain. Her shirt is partially torn.

"Evening, ladies," the woman said. "I'm Vivian."

Startled, the women looked back for only a moment. Kristin and Heather opened their doors and tried to get out.

Vivian lifted a gun that she now has pointing at Jade's head. Kristin and Heather froze in place. "Please don't kill me," Jade said. "I've barely started on my bucket list."

"Back in the car," Vivian said.

Eying the woman, Kristin and Heather got back into the car and closed their doors.

"Take me," Vivian coughed, struggling through her pain. "Take me to your home."

"Whose home?' Heather asked.

"I don't care," Vivian waved her gun and pointed it at Kristin. "Yours."

"You said you didn't care," Jade said.

"Now!"

Kristin put the car in reverse. Vivian sat back in her seat and rode the wave of pain. The car pulled out of the lot and took off up the street.

Kristin unlocked her front door, turned on the light, and entered. Jade and Heather were right behind her, followed by Vivian.

Vivian carried the strap of a duffel over her shoulder and looked to be having a hard time just standing. She shoved the door closed behind her and secured all the locks. Vivian waved the women over to the couch using her gun.

"Sit down."

"You're not well," Kirstin reached into her purse. "Here, let us get you help."

Just as she pulled out her cell phone: Vivian pointed her gun at her. Her hand trembling.

"Put it down!"

Kristin dropped the phone to the floor.

"Now sit!"

The women clung to each other as they sat together on the couch, Heather next to a vase near the end of the table.

Vivian dropped the bag next to a chair across from the window. She closed the curtains and peered around them to the outside.

The women gave each other puzzled looks. Jade looked to the vase and jerked her head at it as a sign for Heather.

Thinking she understood, Heather jerked her head at it.

Jade nodded.

Heather quietly got up, grabbed the vase, and slinked up on Vivian while her back was turned. She was almost there, vase raised and ready to come crashing down on their kidnapper's head.

Vivian spun around and tensed with the gun. "Put it down!"

Heather returned the vase to the end table in a hurry and sat down. "They made me do it."

Kristin and Jade looked at her in shock.

"What?"

"Jade told me to grab the vase."

"You didn't have to do what I said," Jade said.

"Ladies!" Vivian said, snapping the women to attention "I'm starting to wish I was in Victor's company.

"Is that your boyfriend?" Kristin asked.

"No, he's not my boyfriend. Do I look like a vampire?" Vivian plopped down in the chair. "Vampire?" Kristin asked. "I love vampires. You should see my collection of books."

"She really does have just about every book on vampires."

Vivian looked at the women in disbelief. "Out of all the cars I could've broken into, I get the ditz triplets."

"Hey!" Heather said, offended. "I happen to have an IQ of 143."

"It doesn't show, sweet cakes."

Heather's jaw dropped

"Are you saying your boyfriend's a vampire?" Kristin asked.

"He's not my boyfriend! Would I try to kill him if he was?"

"Happens all the time," Jade said.

Vivian grabbed her head as she battled just to stay conscious. "Look, I just need a place to crash until dawn. Then I'll be out of here with the loot."

"Loot?" Heather asked, perking up. "As in cash?"

"How much?" Kristin asked, looking over at the bag then back at Heather.

Vivian picked up her bag and held it to herself in a protective manner. "You three keep your grubby little hands off my money.

"The least you could do is share with us since we're letting you stay here tonight," Heather said.

"You're letting me?" Vivian held up her gun. "Remember my friend here? HE'S letting me stay here."

"Yeah, but we're—"

"Shut up!"

Heather went silent as a dog barked outside in the distance. Vivian looked worried at the noise, getting up with her bag and gun, peering out the window.

"Dogs... they sense things."

"What kind of things?" Heather asked.

"I had a dog once," Jade said. "Gypsy. Kind of a strange name for a boy."

"Not coming from you." Kristin said.

Vivian glanced back, shaking her head in disbelief. The dog barked again and her attention returned to the window.

"Do you like weed?" Jade asked.

"Are you for real?" Vivian asked, puzzled by the question.

"You look like you could use some relaxing," Jade slowly opened her purse. "See? I'm just getting my bag." She pulled out a joint. "I'll share."

Vivian began to cough then choke. The money bag dropped to the floor and all the women eyed it with interest.

Vivian struggled to make it back to her chair, hacking away.

"It doesn't sound like she should be smoking," Heather said.

"I just need my lighter," Jade removed her Zippo from her purse, firing up the joint and then taking a big puff.

She smiled big. "That's what I'm talking about."

"How do you make it at work all day without smoking that shit?"

"I don't. I sneak out to my car every chance I get."

"Maybe we can help you with this Victor," Kristin said, shifting the focus back to Vivian who laughed at her suggestion.

"What makes you think you can take him on when he kicked my ass?"

"There are three of us and only one of you," Heather said.

Vivian laughed so hard that she coughed more. "Have you ever met a vampire?"

The women exchanged looks of puzzlement.

"Of course. I've got a neighbor that goes out looking for blood every night," Heather said, nudging Jade. "Right?"

"Right," Jade said, high as a kite. Then she nudged Kristin.

"Yeah," Kristin added. "He doesn't have a bed and won't let us go down to the basement."

"Do you think I'm stupid?"

"Maybe a little crazy," Heather said under her breath.

"This isn't a laughing matter. They're out there, all over the city. Extorting money from businesses."

"Cool," Jade said.

"Why would vampires need money?" Heather asked.

"That's easy. They live among us and are limited on what kind of night jobs they can get. That's also when they feed so working full-time is rough.

"Thank you for that information, Vampira," Heather said.

Kristin frowned

"I can't believe this is happening," Vivian said, putting both hands to her face.

"So you're saying that bag's full of money," Heather said.

Growing paranoid, Vivian scooted the bag over to herself. She breathed with difficulty, waving her gun at the women.

"You dames stay away from my loot."

"Dames?" Heather asked. "Really?"

"I didn't risk my life going into their lair just to turn my loot over to you three."

"Look, you really need medical attention," Kristin said. "Let me call 9-1-1."

Vivian attempted to respond but lost her breath and began gasping for air. As she struggled more and more, she fell onto the floor. Even in her dire physical condition, she grabbed the bag to protect it.

The gun slipped out of her hand.

Jade took another toke from her joint. While Kristin and Heather watched Vivian intently, unsure of what to do.

Vivian grew still after taking in her last breath.

The women watched her a little longer.

"Is she dead?" Heather asked.

Kristin got up and cautiously approached the body. She kicked the gun away from her. "I think she is."

Heather went over to Vivian and gazed down at her. "Can't say I feel sorry for the bitch. She got what she deserves."

"Come on, Heather," Kristin said. "She didn't deserve this."

"She kidnapped us at gunpoint!"

"She's right," Jade said, giggling.

Kristin grabbed her cell phone from the floor and prepared to dial. "I'm calling the police."

"Wait," Heather eyed the duffel still in Vivian's hands. "Maybe we should see what's in the bag first."

"That's tampering with evidence."

"Then we'll be real careful," she went to the closet, rummaged through it until she found a pair of Kristin's gloves. She returned to Vivian as she put on the gloves.

"What are you doing?"

"Do you want me to leave fingerprints behind?" Heather asked as she took the bag from Vivian's hands, having to struggle a little.

"Come on, Heather. It doesn't matter what's in the bag. A woman is dead on my floor."

Heather laid the bag on the couch and opened it. "We're just taking a look. Chill out."

The first thing she saw inside the bag was cash, a lot of it. Her face illuminated in awe. "The bitch was telling the truth."

Kristin moved to her side for a look, reaching in the bag and taking out a wad of cash.

"Where do you think she got this?"

"From the vampires," Jade giggled. "Weren't you listening?"

"The crazy bitch probably robbed a bank," Heather said. "The cops were after her so she hid in your car."

Heather rummaged through the bag, beyond the cash.

"We have to report this, Heather. It's not ours."

"She didn't strike me much as a religious woman," Heather pulled a large cross out of the bag. She laid the cross aside and pulled out a vial with religious designs on it. "Looks like we have holy water."

She laid that down then her nose scrunched in dislike as she pulled out a necklace made of garlic.

"What the hell?" Heather said, pulling out a mallet and a wooden stake. "Looks like she was planning to kill her boyfriend."

"Maybe that's why she was running with the cash. What if she did?"

"There would be blood on the stake."

"Not if she cleaned it off."

"Yuck," Heather dropped the stake and mallet, disgusted.

"How much do you think is there?" Kristin looked at the money with renewed interest.

"I'd guess a few hundred grand."

"That's a shitload of money," Jade giggled.

"Do you still want to call the police?" Heather said turning to Kristin who looked a lot less decisive than before.

"We... we have to. There's a body in my living room."

Heather put an arm around her shoulders. Both stared at the cash.

"This is true, but we don't have to mention the bag. This crazy woman abducted us at gunpoint and dropped dead after she had us come back here."

"But then we have to lie about what she told us. How she stole the money from the vampires."

"So, we leave that out. Oh, she was ranting about vampires, but we don't mention the bag or money. Deal?"

"I don't know... "

Heather used a pincher grip to pick up the stake and mallet, returning them to the bag along with the other items. She closed the bag and removed the gloves.

"We split the loot three ways," Heather said, gripping Kristin's arms. "Just think what that money can do for us. We can quit our stupid jobs. Maybe we can take a trip to Hawaii.

"I like Hawaii."

"That's my girl," Heather said, now sitting next to Jade.

Jade has finished her joint, her face a picture of bliss.

"Jade, do you understand what we're doing?"

"I'm hungry," Jade started to get up but Heather held her down.

"In a minute. Now remember, the crazy bitch abducted us at gunpoint from the club, made us come back here, ranted about vampires and then died. You don't mention the money."

"What money?"

"I think we're good here," Heather said.

The dog barked again outside the house. He sounded closer than before.

"Something's going on out there," Kristin said.

"Who cares?" Heather said, picking up the bag and holding it to her with a smile. "We got some great things going on in here."

Kristin moved to the window and pulled back the curtain to look outside.

Though the window pane she saw a man. Pale skin, dark clothing. He stared at Kristin from the sidewalk.

"Shit! There's a man outside." Kristin jumped back, the curtain falling back into place.

"Quit playing around."

"I'm serious. He was standing right outside the window."

"Maybe it's the psycho's ex. She didn't rob a bank, she probably stole the loot from him."

"Who carries that kind of money?"

"We do now," Heather said, heading to the stairs and looking back. "And he's getting it back over my dead body."

Kristin watched as Heather jogged up the steps then she returned her attention to the window. She pulled the curtain back again but saw no one there.

"Where did he go"

"You need to start smoking weed," Jade stretched out, relaxing. "It would help you stop being so paranoid."

"I'm not paranoid. "

"That's exactly what I'd expect someone paranoid to say."

Kristin opened her mouth to argue but then heard a noise coming from the back door.

"Did you hear that?"

"Yep," Jade laughed. "But I don't care."

Kristin cautiously made her way toward the kitchen. She nearly stepped on the body she forgot about. She skipped over Vivian and ducked into the kitchen.

Kristin proceeded toward the back door, turned on the light and peered through the window.

Nothing.

Jade laid in a stupor on the floor. A noise at the front door caused her to lift her head.

She watched as the doorknob turned, one way and then back. Very quietly. Driven by curiosity and a false sense of drug induced security, Jade got up and walked over to the door.

Holding the knob, she leaned in closer to the door to listen.

"Hello?" Jade unlocked the door and slowly pulled it open.

The intense looking man stood on the other side, no doubt the "Victor" that Vivian had been talking about.

Jade stared at the vampire, on the verge of panic until snickering.

"Cool," Jade opened the door wider. "Please come in, Mister Vampire."

Victor glid inside, his eyes roaming around the room as Jade closed the door behind him.

"Are you hungry?" Jade asked. "I don't think we have any blood, but I'll see what I can find."

Jade waltzed into the kitchen, snickering.

Kristin still has her eye out the window.

Jade opened the refrigerator, barren except for a few small bottles of juice.

"How do you expect to feed guests?" Jade asked as she started a search through the cabinets.

"Guests? You mean you?"

Jade grabbed an unopened pack of cookies, struggling to open them.

"I'm not a guest. I'm your friend. And you say I get stupid when I'm high."

Jade ripped open the pack of cookies and they went flying.

"Oopsie," she gathered the cookies from the counter and popped one into her mouth.

"What guest are you talking about?" Kristin asked, moving in closer.

"The vampire man," Jade said, turning for the doorway.

Panicked, Kristin shoved Jade back and hurried past her.

"Hey!" Jade called out. "Not very nice."

She juggled several cookies in her arms and followed Kristin.

Kristin walked into the living room very slowly, her eyes searching.

"You ran him off, didn't you?" Jade asked as Heather came down the steps without the bag of money.

"Ran who off?" Heather asked.

"The vampire man."

"He's inside the house," Kristin said.

"You believe that? Geez, Kristin," Heather snatched a cookie from Jade and took a bite.

"Hey, get your own."

"I just did," Heather said, turning to Kristin. "She's not all there. Not like she ever is."

"I heard that."

"I know," Heather said, strolling off to the kitchen. Jade followed while Kristin moved to the main door and found the deadbolt locked.

Still troubled, she looked up the stairs as she followed after her friends.

Heather got a wine cooler from the refrigerator and took a sip.

Jade gobbled down some of the spilt cookies.

"He's after the bag," Kristin said, entering the kitchen.

"The asshole will never find it."

Kristin hugged herself as she looked back to the hall.

Heather walked over, touched her shoulder and Kristin nearly jumped out of her skin.

"Jesus! What's wrong with you?"

"I have this bad feeling," Kristin said.

"It's all those stupid books you read," Heather said, now taking a seat at the table. "Try Shakespeare. He's actually very soothing for a dead guy."

"His hair was black," Kristin said, turning to Heather with fear on her face.

"So?" Heather pulled out her cell phone and texted while she sipped from her drink.

"Vampires have black hair."

"They do!"

"I never did understand that," Heather said. "How many people walk around with hair that dark? But all of the classic vampires have black hair. Don't they bite redheads or redheads? Or does everyone's hair turn black when they become a vampire?"

"What if she wasn't crazy?" Kristin hurriedly sat down next to Heather.

"Are you serious? There's no such things as vampires."

"Yeah, you're right"

"Maybe he's a goth," Jade said.

"Dammit," Heather said, taking a long swig from her wine cooler then stopping. She got up without the bottle and left her cell phone on the table. "That stuff just goes right through me."

Heather went into the bathroom and closed the door.

"Know where I can get more weed?" Jade said, abandoning her cookies.

Kristin returned her attention to the back window lost in thought.

"Kristin?"

"Yeah," Kristin turned and faced Jade. "I'll let you in on a secret if you promise not to tell anyone."

"A secret?"

"Do you promise?"

"Cross my heart and hope to die," Jade happily crossed her heart. "Stick a needle in my eye."

"Okay, okay," Kristin said. "No need for the ghastly visuals."

"What's your secret?"

Kristin looks over to the closed bathroom door, then to Jade. "You know how I act like I hate pot and pretend to never smoke it?"

"That's not a secret," Jade said in disappointment as she began to walk away.

"I love smoking it."

"Really?" Jade turned back, happiness streaking across her face.

"I even have a baggie stashed in the trunk of my car. I'll split it with you if you get it."

"Is it a quarter?"

"Two. One for each of us."

"Cool! Where are your keys?"

Kristin located her keys inside her purse and dropped them into Jade's outstretched hand.

"I'll be back," she said. "How many times do you hear people say that and never return?" "How about saying you won't be back?" Kristin asked.

"Oooh! Like opposite day. I like it," Jade said, opening the front door. "I won't be back."

She laughed as she stepped outside and closed the door behind her.

"That's the idea," Kristin hurried to double-check the door locks, securing those that are not fastened. Laughing, she steps outside and closes the door behind her. Kristin hurries to double-check the door locks. She secured those not fastened. She then ran to the front window and looked out.

Jade opened Kristin's trunk. She rummaged through the few items inside - blanket, cooler, CDs, jacket. No weed. She even looked inside the cooler and searched the jacket pockets.

"Where the hell's the weed?"

Kristin clung to the drapes as she watched Jade with anticipation.

Jade closed the trunk and returned to the house.

Kirstin stood in place as the door jiggled with Jade attempting to open it.

"Let me in," Jade called out.

Kristin waited until the noise stepped. She stepped up to the door and waited on pins and needles.

"Boo!"

Kristin spun around, a hand over her racing heart.

"You should see your face," Jade laughed.

"Dammit, Jade. How did you get in?" Kristin stepped away, needing to hold herself up with a hand on the couch back.

"The back door was unlocked."

"I locked it."

"Apparently you didn't." Jade closed in. "And that's what you get for sending me on a wild goose chase."

The vampire suddenly appeared behind Kristin.

"Oh hi, Mister Vampire!" Jade said.

Kristin eyes widened, she turned around quick to look behind herself.

No one there.

"Stop it with the vampire shit!" Kristin said, shoving Jade.

"Fine, but don't yell for me when he sucks the blood right out of you," Jade said, jogging up the steps.

Kristin leaned against the couch to steady herself.

"What's Jade yelling about now?" Heather stepped out of the bathroom and joined Kristin.

"She caught me eating her cookies and freaked," Kristin said.

"I'm telling you, smoking weed day and night isn't good on a body. I had a boyfriend once who did that shit and he kept calling me Linda in bed. His mind was fried."

"Or he was hung up on an ex-girlfriend."

"Look at this body," Heather said, taking a sexy pose. "How could any man be hung up on someone else?"

"I see your point," Kristin held back laughter, containing it to a snicker.

"Laughter," Heather said, taking Kristin by the arm. "Now that's more like it. What you need is a fun-filled day with me."

Heather led Kristin to the couch and laid an arm around her shoulders as they sat.

"Picture this. We both go into work tomorrow and tell our bosses to fuck off. You come by the call center and pick me up. We shop until we drop and have lunch. Hell, we can even see a movie, but I get to pick."

"Sounds nice."

"I'll even let Jade come along, but she can't bring weed with her. I'm not doing time after my life just took a turn for the better."

Heather looked back toward the kitchen.

"Where is Jade anyway?"

Jade's voice carried down from the upstairs. "Here you are. I'm afraid I got some bad news for you."

"Who is she talking to?" Heather asked.

Kristin shook her head.

They both got up and ascended the stairs, pausing as they reached the top.

They realize that Jade's voice was coming from the spare bedroom, with the door only open a crack to a darkened room.

"Not much of talker are you?" they heard Jade's voice again. "Just so you know, I believe in vampires. Do you like cookies?"

Heather pushed open the door and turned on the light.

Jade stood near the bed, facing away from the door. She turned around pissed.

"You scared him off," Jade said. "He hates bright light."

"I think she's gone off the deep end," Heather said.

Kristin, trailing behind Heather, noticed movement near the steps. She saw a shadow of the vampire man, looming near the stairs.

"Jade," Kristin began. "Do you know where I keep my takeout menus?"

"Top drawer in the kitchen."

"Go ahead and choose a place. I wouldn't mind having some pizza."

"This late?" Heather asked.

"I love pizza!" Jade bounced out of the room.

Unaware of the danger, Jade went to the stairs.

Victor lunged out of the darkness like a spider after an insect in his web, grabbing Jade.

The young woman fell to the ground, screaming as Heather watched in horror.

Kristin pushed her into the spare room, slamming the door closed.

Heather shoved a chair under the door knob and searched her pockets.

"Where's my phone?"

"I don't know."

"Where's yours?"

"On the charger in my room."

"Just great! Have you forgotten there's a dead woman in your living room? What a time to charge your phone."

"The battery was dead."

"Poor Jade," Heather paced back and forth. "On the bright side, that's one less taking a share of my money."

"YOUR money?"

"I'm the one looking after it."

"I don't recall nominating you."

"Do you have a problem with me, Kristin?" Heather said, stepping in the face of her friend.

"You just took over the money without any discussion. How do I know I can trust you?"

"I thought I could trust you," Heather folded her arms. "The door swings both ways."

A large slam coming from downstairs startled both women.

Heather clung to Kristin's arm as they listened in silence.

"Maybe he left."

"Why don't you go look?" Kristin asked.

"Oh, no you don't. We're going together."

Heather moved the chair away from the door and gripped Kristin's arm.

They open the door and Jade suddenly appeared, startling them both.

Jade held her head, her legs unsteady.

"What happened?" she asked.

"Your playmate bashed your head against the wall."

"He wouldn't do that."

Kristin took a close look at both sides of Jade's neck. Heather and Jade looked at her inquisitively.

"Just checking."

"She'd be pale. Geez, Kristin. I thought you were an expert."

Kristin smirked at her as they both go down the hall and to the top of the steps.

Unable to see anything below in the dark, they made their way down.

Reaching the bottom of the stairs, Kristin turned to look all around the living room. The front door was open and the women just stared at it in anxiousness.

"For Heaven's sake," Heather turned on the main light and stormed past Kristin and Jade to the door, closing it. "Grow some balls."

"But we're girls."

Heather turned around, ready to make a sarcastic comment. Instead, panic came to her face as she saw Victor looming behind the unsuspecting Kristin and Jade.

"Behind you!"

Kristin and Jade spun around to look.

Victor clamped a strong hand around Kristin's throat. Kristin quickly struggled to breathe. "You foolish mortal," Victor hissed. "You think you can stab a vampire in the back and get away with it? You've got the wrong side."

"You're hurting my friend" Jade said, trying to pry the vampire's hand loose. "Play nice!"

Victor backhanded Jade, sending her flying back to the couch.

Then the vampire flung Kristin to the floor, leaving her there gasping for air.

Victor turned his attention to Heather. As he approached her, Heather stumbled into things in her path as she attempted to keep her distance.

"Where is my money?"

"Money? We don't know what you're talking about."

"I think he means the money that girl—"

"Zip it, Jade!" Heather said.

They watched as Victor paused next to Vivian on the floor, looking at her with contempt. "This foolish girl thought he could defeat me. You see what happened to her. If you want a different fate, you'll hand over the money, NOW!"

"Come on!" Kristin bolted to her feet and pulled Heather along with her to the main door. Jade got to her feet but stood back and watched.

Victor mysteriously appeared at the door to block their exit, the women then change course for the front door.

And found Victor standing there, blocking their way out again.

The only place left was the stairs and the two girls raced up the steps.

Victor then turned his attention to Jade.

She didn't seem afraid but then had a change of heart, running up the steps to be with her friends.

Kristin and Heather ran into the spare bedroom, locking the door behind themselves.

"How did he keep popping up everywhere?" Heather asked.

"Vampires are fast."

"He's not a freaking vampire"

"Then what is he?"

"I don't know. Maybe a dude wacked out on PCP."

The two women shuddered as they heard a pounding on the door, clinging to each other.

"Let me in!" Jade screamed.

"No way!" Heather said.

Jade heard a creak on the stairs and slowly turned her head to look. A shadow crept along the wall as the owner grew closer.

Victor arrived at the top, studied Jade for a moment and snarled, showing his fangs.

He walked slowly toward her.

Jade pounded harder on the door while keeping an eye on Victor.

"Open the door!"

Kristin and Heather do nothing, listening at the door.

"He's coming!"

Kristin and Heather heard a thud in the hall followed by a long silence. Heather stood frozen with fear, Kristin bit her finger nails staring at the door knob.

Her self-preservation in mind, Heather opened the closet and unburied the bag in the top under a stack of blankets.

Kristin finally tore her attention away from the main door.

"Great hiding place," Kristin said. "He would never find it there."

Heather ignored the statement, setting the bag down on the bed.

"What are you doing?" Kristin asked.

"You have an intruder messed up on drugs in your house," Heather said, pulling out the stake and mallet, looking at the items with awe. "It's time we defend ourselves."

"I thought you don't believe he's a vampire."

"I'm going for the head."

Kristin reached into the bag and pulled out the necklace of garlic, putting it around her own neck.

"Really?" Heather asked.

"Not taking chances here," Kristin said.

"All we have to do is make it to your room and get your phone," Heather said, walking to the door. "The police station is two minutes away. Are you with me?"

Kristin looked unsure, but nodded. She grabbed the bottle of holy water and the cross from the bag then joined Heather at the door. The stench of Kristin's garlic necklace caused Heather to turn away. "I'll never be able to get that smell out of the cash," Heather said, as she moved the chair out of the way, unlocked the door, and opened it slowly.

Both expected to see the intruder on the other side. No sign of him. They proceed cautiously into the hall then entered Kristin's bedroom, turning on the light.

Kristin locked the door behind them. Heather looked to the night stand, then the dresser.

"Where's your phone?" Heather asked.

"Oh, it's in the spare bedroom."

"You mean the one we just left?"

"No, the other one."

"You said it was in this one! Why can't you make up your mind?!"

"I don't know, Heather. Maybe I don't want us to get help. Maybe I want us to be vampires so we can live happily ever after, forever!"

Heather looked at her in disbelief. "You've lost it."

"I don't handle stress well."

A hand reached out from under the bed and grabbed Heather's ankle. She screamed as she tried to get free, causing Kristin to scream.

Jade climbed out from under the bed.

"You shit!" Heather screamed, giving Jade a hard shove.

"Ow!" Jade said.

"She's like a boomerang," Kristin said.

"I had to hide somewhere since you guys wouldn't let me in."

"Since you left your phone in the wrong room," Heather turned to Kristin "You go get it."

"I... I can't go out there."

"Oh, you're going," Heather pulled Kristin by the arm to the door but Kristin dropped to the floor.

Unconscious, with the cross and holy water dropping down next to her.

"Now look what you did."

"She's faking," Heather said, kicking Kristin in the leg. "That was pathetic. Get up."

Kristin remained motionless on the floor. Annoyed with her, Heather stooped by her side and tried to pull Kristin up.

"Come on, Kristin. Stop playing around."

Heather sighed and got back up.

"Okay fine," she said. "If you want something done, do it yourself."

Taking the stake and mallet, Heather opened the door and stepped out.

Jade turned her back to Kristin to watch.

"Where are you going?"

"To a party. Want to come?"

Jade's face lit up and started to respond until Heather disappeared down the hall.

Kristin lifted her head up, watching Heather leave.

Heather entered the dark bedroom and turned on the light. No cell phone on a charger here. She grinned deliriously, unaware that Victor stood behind her.

The vampire snarled and Heather spun around, lifting the stake too late.

Victor snatched the stake and mallet from her hands, flinging them aside.

Heather moved for the door but Victor headed her off.

She moved in the opposite direction and Victor stayed with her.

"I... I don't have your money," Heather said, crying quietly as she backed away. "Kristin's got it! Go talk to her."

Victor backed her into a corner and looked at the human with contempt.

"You mortals are pathetic. I can smell a rat a mile away.. and that's clearly you."

He bared his fangs as Heather's eyes widened in terror.

Jade clung to the open door as she listened to Heather's scream. She closed and locked the door as Kristin bounced up as if nothing was ever wrong with her.

"She got Heather."

"Yeah, that's a shame," Kristin unlocked and opened the door, took a cautious look out and left. Jade hurried out after her.

"Wait for me!"

Kristin ran to the spare bedroom and closed the door in a hurry.

Jade caught it in time and pushed her way in.

Then Kristin closed and locked the door.

"I thought we were friends," Jade said.

"Yeah, well, money's thicker than blood," Kristin said, looking over at the money bag in awe. She pulled some cash out of the bag and smelled it, smiling big.

Jade watched her, something clicking in her thoughts.

"You're after the money."

"What? It's OUR money."

"Then let me have my half," Jade said, holding out her hand.

"No!" Kristin hurriedly returned the money to the bag, clutching the duffel to her body.

"You set me up," Jade said, getting in her face. "Then you faked fainting so Heather would go look for your phone that wasn't even there!"

Kristin bumped onto the edge of the bed, shaking her head. "No, you've got it all wrong."

"Do I, Kristin? I don't think so."

A loud thump at the door startled both women.

Thinking fast, Kristin held the bag to her and rushed to the door.

Jade chased after her, knowing what she was about to do.

"No, don't!" Jade said.

Kristin opened the door, Victor standing on the other side.

Jade tried to get behind the door but Kristin pushed her out into the open.

Victor raced inside, plowing into Jade.

They fell back on the bed, Victor on top. He closed in on Jade's neck with his fangs.

"No!" Jade screamed as Kristin dashed out of the room with the duffel.

Kristin rushed inside the spare bedroom and stopped. She saw Heather lying on the floor, two punctures on her throat, the color drained from her skin. The mallet and stake laid off to the side. Kristin hurried to hide the bag in the top of the closet. She swooped up the weapons and turned for the door.

Victor stood in the doorway, blood dripping from his mouth. He wiped it away with the back of his arm.

"Midnight snacks are to die for," he sneered.

Kristin's grip tightened on the sharp wooden stake.

"Now, give me my money or you're next," Victor stepped to her.

Kristin wasted no time yelling out as she charged Victor, plowing into the vampire.

Both fell back to the floor with Kristin on top. She angrily pounded the stake into Victor's heart with several hits.

Exhausted, Kristin began chuckling deliriously.

She pulled her cell phone out of her pocket and dialed 9-1-1 as she sat back against the wall.

"Yes, some couple hopped up on drugs broke into my house. They attacked me and my friends. I think both may be dead... Kristin Reynolds. 492 Peyton Place. Please hurry."

She hung up the phone and grinned.

Kristin hurried into the spare bedroom and went to the closet. She took the bag of money out and opened it on the bed.

She ran her hands through the stacks of money, smiling as big as humanly possible, hearing the sirens in the distance.

Kristin shoved the money back inside and zipped it up.

Picking up the bag, she didn't see Heather and Jade standing behind her.

Kristin just heard a snarl.

Her eyes wide, she turned and saw something different about them. Pale skin. Black eyes.

She screamed when she saw their fangs.

END

VAMPIRE ROCKERS

RAY DURAN

49

Harold Liebling looked to be in his mid-thirties. He wore wire glasses, winged tipped shoes and a fedora. A journalist by trade, he could not think of anything else he wanted to do with his life. When he dies and goes to hell, he just hoped they had keyboards so he could type up his stories.

He watched as a gust of wind pushed a leaf past a line of headstones. The leaf stopped outside a crypt that had dates from the 1800s stamped above.

Liebling closed the iron gate of the crypt shut.

When he originally began doing the article, there was no way he could imagine how far it could take him. Or how long.

He took out a small note pad from his rumpled trenchcoat and pulled a pencil off his ear, jotting something down.

Liebling prided himself on having a news hawk's promise to his readers. To follow all leads to hell and back if he had to.

He heard a clicking noise and stopped reading. The noise came from the crypt.

CHAPTER ONE

Liebling stopped tapping the keys of his computer keyboard, leaned back in his office chair and looked at the bulletin board above his desk.

Old newspaper articles were paired together. There was one about an all-girl 1800s era classic ensemble called "Easy Street," with a mystery illness that infected thousands. Another about an all-female 1920s jazz quartet called "Luster," with warnings of the Spanish flu epidemic. One girl looked a lot like one of the girls in "Easy Street."

Another article, in color, showed a group of girl singers calling themselves "Savvy" attending a 1960s pop concert. Again, one of the girls looked like the same one from the other two bands.

Another showed disco women in satin hot pants announcing an appearance at a club, along with a magazine article on Aids. One of the women is named "Rayne", and yes she looked a lot like the same girl in all the band's photos.

Liebling looked down on his computer.

On the screen, he's brought up a press release notice from the band "Black Chalice" that they were currently auditioning new singers in advance of a sophomore album and world tour.

"Well, well, well, you found yourself another one," he whispered.

Liebling hit the PRINT button just as a piercing screeched erupted from the printer.

CHAPTER TWO

The guitar amp screeched as the band Black Chalice cracked into a fast, alternative rock song on their stage set.

Morgan had short punk hair and always wore sport bras which showed off her biceps and shoulders. She pounded on the drum kit with savage fury.

Eden had long flowing hair, funky eye shadow and red lipstick. She wore a man's plaid shirt, slacks and work boots. She played lead guitar.

Fawn never wore make up. A jeans, t-shirt and sneakers girl, she plucked the strings of her bass guitar.

Rayne stood at the center. Pale with long, luxurious hair. She wore a black Victorian era dress, black heels, and ran her delicate black finger-nailed hands over the keys of a standup keyboard.

Rayne shook her head, disturbed. She glanced over at Eden and stepped up to the mic stand.

"Stop! Stop! Stop!" Rayne yelled into the mic.

The music ground to a halt. Fawn grabbed a water bottle of her amp and drank.

"It's too fast," Rayne said.

"That's how it goes, bitch," Eden replied.

Rayne's eyes burned with fury, but they cooled as she turned to address Eden.

"But that's not the way it has to. I showed you yesterday how it can-"

"Fuck you, you're out," Eden took off her guitar and laid it in its case.

"Eden!" Morgan said.

"Call up that broad from-what's their name? The Runaways tribute."

"Give her a chance, Eden," Fawn pleaded.

Eden snapped the case closed, picked it up and strutted over to Fawn. "Whose band is this?"

"Yours," Fawn looked away, submissive.

Eden moved past Rayne without looking at her and stepped off the stage.

"You said we could try new stuff," Morgan called out.

Eden stopped but did not turn around.

"And that you'd consider doing anything if it meant bringing us all the way to the top," Fawn added.

Eden slowly turned around. "Is this really what you guys want?"

Fawn drank more water while Morgan nervously twiddled her drum sticks.

"You don't have to do what she says just because she let us rehearse in her house," Eden continued.

"All I'm asking is to give it a try," Rayne said, her voice soothing.

Eden looked at Rayne and found her staring right back.

"I promise that once you let these melodies loose from their chains you'll see how they'll just magically float over your beautiful, heart felt lyrics and-"

Rayne's words seemed to do exactly that to Eden, who suddenly relaxed as if she were in a trance.

"-Caress everyone's soul," Raven said.

Eden blinked out of it and grew hard again. "Nice try, Florence Nightingale, but I want to fuck their soul, not caress it."

Eden stormed past Rayne and crossed the empty, dusty room to the door. She stepped out without saying another word.

"She'll be back," Morgan said.

"I know," said Rayne.

Fawn took off her bass guitar and stood it against her amp. "I have to pee, Where's the-"

"Upstairs, end of hall."

As Fawn nodded thanks and crossed to the staircase, Rayne moved back to the keyboard and started playing a haunting, classical inspired piece.

"That's cool," Morgan said.

"It's your song."

"What?"

"That's what I was telling you guys. See how beautiful it can be?" Rayne said.

"Wow."

Morgan started playing a jazzy roll on the snare. Rayne looked over to her, grinned and continued to play.

CHAPTER THREE

Fawn reached the upstairs hallway of Rayne's house. She scrunched her nose at the peeling wallpaper and chipped paint on the walls as she made her way down the hall.

At the end of the hall, she saw two doors.

She opened the one on the right. Looking inside, she saw more of a lair than a bedroom. Reds and blacks on the walls, four-poster bed, antique furnishings, closet full of women's clothes that looked like it belonged to an era long gone.

And an old phonograph on the table.

"Cool," Fawn said.

She entered the room and crossed over to the phonograph. There's a vintage record platter on it by a classical group called "Easy Street.

Seeing the slipcover for it, she picked it up and scrutinized it.

The aged cover showed four women and the singer looked exactly like Rayne.

"Whoa!"

The music from downstairs suddenly stopped. Then Fawn heard a crash of cymbals.

She rushed down the stairs and found Rayne helping a woozy Morgan away from her collapsed drum kit.

"What happened?"

"She'll be fine," Rayne assured.

"Morgan?"

Morgan glanced at Fawn. She's pale, shaky, and weak. "I'll be fine. I-I just need to lie down.."

Rayne put an arm around Morgan and helped her shuffle past Fawn up the stairs. Morgan limped.

As they passed Fawn, Rayne looked at her with an unblinking, steady gaze.

Fawn wrapped her arms around herself as if she suddenly got cold and stepped away.

CHAPTER FOUR

Rayne helped Morgan lie down on the bed, then sauntered to the phonograph and turned it on.

The scratchy classical music has the same melody as the music she was playing on the keyboard.

"How hard do you think it will be to convince Eden?"

"About you joining?" Morgan asked. "Like pushing a square peg through a round hole."

Rayne glided across the room to the closet and studied the black leather and lace clothing hanging on hooks.

"The band is all she has," Morgan continued. "Ever since Candy was killed she feels the need to protect us. Mother us."

"Smother you."

"What?"

Rayne took a black leather corset down and then pulled a matching mini-skirt off a hook.

"I'm just saying I know where she's coming from. My last band was pretty close too."

Rayne carried the clothes to the bed and dropped them near Morgan's feet.

"You really think this is going to help us?"

"It can't hurt, right?"

Rayne stared at Morgan. She spotted a trickle of blood on her upper thigh.

"You're bleeding. We need to take care of that."

Rayne headed for her bureau when she heard a knock at the door.

CHAPTER FIVE

Fawn opened the front door and saw the smiling Liebling wearing an alternative rock band shirt, jeans and deck shoes.

"Is this where the band is?" he asked.

"No," Fawn said and shut the door in his face.

Liebling checked the address on his cell phone, looked around the area and knocked again.

"Go away," Fawn yelled out.

"I'm Harold Liebling. Harry-from Skull Ring Magazine?"

"Never heard of it!"

"We're new. I'm doing an article-"

"Fuck off!"

Liebling sighed and tapped the phone against his other hand. "Is there someone else I can talk to? My editor already cleared this with you guys."

Fawn opened the door. Liebling looked past her and saw the band's gear set up on the stage in the background.

"There's supposed to be no press until after we pick -"

Liebling entered the home, forcing Fawn to take a step back.

"Is she here?"

"Who?"

Liebling looked around the room. "Have you guys started yet?"

"Look, mister, I think you need to wait until Eden gets back.

Fawn pushed Liebling back but he doesn't budge.

"These rehearsals are private and-"

"It's okay, Fawn," Rayne called out. "He's okay."

Fawn looked over to the stairs and saw Rayne at the top, partially hidden in the shadows.

"So you found-us," Rayne said.

Liebling stepped further inside for a better look at Rayne, but she slipped back deeper into the shadows.

"Yep. There's no escape."

Fawn gave a 'what the hell are you talking about?' look that Liebling picked up on.

"We've been wanting to do a story on you guys for awhile now."

"Really?" Fawn asked. "Nobody told me."

"Which one are you?"

"What?"

"In the band."

"Bass."

"Then there you have it," Liebling moved past Fawn toward the stage.

"What the hell does that mean?"Fawn asked as she followed Liebling.

CHAPTER SIX

The haunting classic music continued to play as Morgan admired herself in a full-length mirror. The corset and mini-skirt have made her a hundred times sexier.

"This isn't me. I don't have the body for it."

"Nonsense," Rayne said coming behind her.

Morgan whirled around, startled by Rayne's closeness as she couldn't be seen in the mirror.

"Its perfect," Rayne said.

Morgan returned to looking at her reflection in the mirror and grinned at herself.

"It is pretty sick, huh?"

Rayne still couldn't be seen in the mirror.

Fawn exited the kitchen area carrying a can of beer and a glass of water. She handed the water to Liebling.

"What was that last question again?"

"If any of you-"

"Oh yeah, right. No, none of us are married or have kids. At least I don't think so. Never can tell with super slut," Fawn nodded up at the ceiling. "Morgan's screwed everything with a dick from here to New York and back again twice."

Liebling typed on his phone.

"What are you doing?"

"Making notes."

"Don't write that."

Liebling stopped typing and looked at Fawn.

"About New York. We've never actually played there yet."

Liebling smirked and returned to tapping.

"Holy shit!" Fawn said.

"What?"

Fawn moved past Liebling and stopped as Rayne and Morgan stepped off the stairs and approached.

Morgan's limp was gone and besides the corset and mini-skirt, she now wore fishnet stockings and Doc Marten boots. Her hair was now spiked, her lipstick black and skull earrings dangled from her ears.

"You like?" Morgan asked.

Fawn gave Rayne a queer look "Now you're going to turn us all into Dragon Tattoo, is that it?"

Rayne raised her hands in surrender. "Hey, I only made a suggestion."

"It's true, Fawn. This was my idea."

"A friggin stupid one," Fawn said.

Rayne lasered a look at Liebling

"What do you think Harold?"

"Truth? I think it looks kinda cool."

Morgan grinned.

"He doesn't count," Fawn said.

Rayne sighed.

"I'll tell you right now, when Eden comes back she's going to go Terminator on your ass."

Rayne sighed. "Can we take this off campus?" She flicked her head at Liebling and then headed for the kitchen. Fawn clued in and followed.

"Sorry about that," Morgan said.

Liebling waved his hand as if to say that it didn't bother him and watched the girls enter the kitchen.

"Rayne tells me you were after her for years," Morgan said.

"What else did she tell you?"

"That now you're here to-"

A crash of dishes and the sound of cutlery falling to the floor came from the kitchen.

"Sorry," Rayne cried out. "My bad!"

CHAPTER SEVEN

The sun came up behind Eden as she swayed to the door. Drunk as a skunk, she fell down and slowly got back up, brushing the gravel off her knees. She stared at the door knocker, a silver bust of a gargoyle head on polished onyx plinth. She didn't want to touch the damn thing, so instead she pounded on the door.

No response.

Then she kicked it. Once. Then three more times.

"Come on, bitches, open up. I know you're still here. I see your cars."

The door opened a crack. Eden pushed it wide and stumbled in.

The hallway smelled of cooking and dust. The sun angled through the stained glass skylight above the front door and cast a pattern on the wallpaper like a demonic gargoyle with horns sticking out.

The drapes were drawn but the instruments and stage remained intact. Then she saw movement to her left.

Fawn scampered out of the light into the darkness of a corner by the stairs.

Eden squinted her eyes and saw that Fawn now had poofed out hair, black makeup, a mesh shirt, leather pants and matching boots.

"What the shit is going on here?" Eden said.

As the door opened, the intruding light traced a moving line on the floor heading for Liebling in his chair. He stood and stepped away from it just as it reached him.

"Who the hell are you?" Eden asked.

Morgan exited the kitchen gnawing at a chicken leg. "We're being interviewed."

"Oh yeah?

Eden lurched further into the room and Fawn rushed out of the shadows to slam the door shut.

"Harry Liebling," he said offering his hand to Eden. "Skull Ring Magazine."

Eden ignored Liebling and stared at Morgan, then turned around to look at Fawn.

"Didn't take long for her to convert you two, did it?"

"It's not like that, Eden," Morgan said.

"Then tell me what it's like, Morgan, because Halloween is six months away and you've never been one to play dress up."

"It is dress-up, Eden," Fawn said.

"Huh?"

"We could go on stage naked and it wouldn't matter."

"Right."

"What she means is that what we wear on the outside is just a shell. It doesn't change what we feel inside. What we are inside."

Liebling moved closer to the girls. "From what I've heard this is to be a completely new vision for the band."

"I didn't say I wanted a 'completely new vision," Eden said.

"Was what you were doing before working okay for you?"

"Yeah," Eden said. "We had steady gigs. A decent CD. West Coast tour opening for Crappy Day."

"But wouldn't you want Crappy Day opening for you? An album at the top of the charts?"

Eden wobbled over to the stage. "There is no way in hell she can promise that."

"That's right-she can't," Fawn said.

"But if we all remain united and stick to one path," said Morgan.

"There's no limit to what we can and accomplish and -"

"I can help you get there," Liebling said.

Eden took her time looking at each one of them, then plunked her butt down on the edge of the stage.

"How?"

First Fawn smiled, then Morgan, then Liebling as they moved toward Eden.

Liebling sat in a large velour armchair and helped himself to a bottle of whiskey on the table. He shuddered as he drank it and it burned his throat. But it warmed him up as he moved to one side of Eden, while Morgan cuddled next to her.

Fawn sat on the floor and began petting Eden's leg.

"I start with a series of interviews with each of you, staggering the release to draw up publicity. The more issues I can get you into, the more Black Chalice's name spreads."

"And then what?

Morgan ran a hand through Eden's hair while Fawn kept stroking her leg.

"The rest is up to us, baby," Morgan said.

CHAPTER EIGHT

A candle lit the room as Rayne slept on her back. A tap on the door and her eyes popped open.

Fawn stuck her head inside from around the opening door.

"Sorry to wake you, but I think she's ready."

Rayne sat up, swung her legs over and got out of bed as Fawn pulled Eden in by the hand. Morgan followed.

"You're okay with this?"

"I guess so," Eden said.

Rayne got close to Eden. "No guessing. This only works if we're all one-hundred percent committed as a team. A band."

"I am. Let's do it."

Rayne nodded and waved her hand for Fawn and Morgan to bring Eden over to the bed. As they sat Eden down on the edge, Rayne continued onto the closet.

"Any preference?" Rayne asked.

Eden looked up at Fawn and Morgan and then over at Rayne.

"You mean me?" Eden asked. "Preference for what?"

Rayne sorted through the black clothing. "Leather? Lace? Fringe, no fringe? Solid, mesh, see-through?"

Rayne took down a vintage Victorian era dress in one hand and a sexy, shiny, plastic mini-dress in the other.

"Old school or new school?"

"Oh, gee, I don't know. Whatever you think."

Rayne hung the Victorian dress back up and approached the bed with the plastic mini-dress.

"Let's see how this looks," Rayne said.

Eden stood and started to unbutton her shirt. Fawn helped and Morgan unbuckled Eden's belt.

"Whoa, guys, I got this."

Fawn and Morgan looked to Rayne.

Rayne nodded her assent and the girls back off. Eden stripped down to her underwear and bra.

"Lie down," Rayne said.

"Why? I thought I was-"

"We're not quite ready."

Eden let herself be laid on the bed by Fawn while Rayne crossed to her bureau and took out a bottle of nail polish.

As Morgan circled to the other side of the bed and sat, Rayne arrived and sat on the bed at Eden's feet.

"What are you doing?" Eden asked.

Rayne unscrewed the cap and took out the brush.

"Just going for the full effect." Rayne lifted one of Eden's feet and put it in her lap. She started to pain black polish on the toes. "They want us to die. To go away screaming in the night with a stake in our heart. Just fade away like a photograph exposed to sunlight like there was nothing there to begin with. But what I want is fame. Not jut temporary fame but an eternal one."

Fawn sat on the bed near Eden's head

Morgan slid closer.

Eden closed her eyes and relaxed. After a beat, they suddenly popped open and screamed as-

Rayne buried herself in between Eden's thighs.

Eden squirmed and tried to get away but Fawn and Morgan held her down.

"Oh my God, what are you doing?" Eden screamed. "Stop. Get away from me."

Rayne lifted her head to give a blaming look to Fawn. Blood dripped off two long, sharp fangs.

"Hold her still," Rayne lowered her mouth back to the femoral artery in one of Eden's thighs and sucked.

"It's okay, baby," Fawn said.

Eden laid spread-eagled, her thighs splattered with blood. *She's killing me. This bitch is killing me,* she thought.

The feeling of terror and helplessness was too much for her to overcome. Already she felt lifeless, already she felt the darkness drawing her in but the at the same time she was acutely conscious of the fangs being dug into her upper thigh. She felt the warm blood being sucked out of her body.

She saw Rayne's head bobbing and dipping between her legs. The pumping of her blood unstoppable.

Eden resistance waned. She stopped thrashing.

"It'll all be over soon," Morgan said.

As Fawn and Morgan stroked and caressed Eden, Rayne continued to both give and receive.

CHAPTER NINE

Liebling looked around the the room, with brightly illuminated display cases of silver jewelry and artistically arranged shelves of occult books. The walls were lined in black felt, the floor black-carpeted.

There were no windows.

A CD player stood prominently in the center of the room and Liebling pushed play. He noticed the CD case for "Black Chalice" atop it and picked it up.

All the girls are on it with Rayne front and center just like her other albums.

The music started with a haunting keyboard leading the band into a goth rock song with that familiar melody and Rayne begins to sing.

Liebling picked up a piece of paper, finding a push pin and tacking it on the bulletin board.

The paper is a print out of the article of Black Chalice he wrote for Skull Ring titled "Goth Rock Ladies Ready To Take On The World By Hell Or High Water."

On Liebling's computer is a newspaper story about the rising number of infection cases infecting people on the West coast possibly linked to West Nile virus.

CHAPTER TEN

Backstage, the girls listened to the waiting crowd.

They chant, "We want Black Chalice" over and over.

Rayne motioned for the band to huddle together. "This is it, ladies. What we've been waiting an eternity for. Are you ready to rock?"

Morgan grinned, showing long and sharp fangs. "I'm ready."

"Are you ready to spread the word?" Rayne asked.

Fawn grinned. Her fangs glistened in the light. "Ready."

Rayne looked at Eden who's busy fiddling with a fingernail. "Eden?"

"Yeah, yeah, I'm ready." Eden smirked, her fangs ready to go. "Let's do this."

The girls all clapped and headed for the curtain separating the back stage area with the stage itself.

As they passed through the curtain the excitement of the crowd increased with cheers and applause.

"Ladies and gentleman, please welcome-Black Chalice!"

The crowd cheered and then seconds later, the haunting melody started to play.

"Are you ready, sisters?" Rayne asked. "You know what to do. On three. One...two...three!"

The four girls ran onto the stage.

And into the crowd. Snarling. Biting.

The happy, excited cheers turned to cries of horror.

Eden was the first to attack. She bit into the face of a man sitting in the front row, wearing their band's t-shirt. Her fangs crunched against his cheekbone and he screamed. Then Fawn held him down and Eden sank her teeth deep into his throat.

The crowd screeched but the music held them strangely in place.

Rayne stared into the audience from behind her microphone as she played the keyboard. Her face was unblinking and intense.

"Don't resist it," Rayne said. "Let it wash over you like a soothing wave."

The audience screamed as their necks were ripped out. Rayne just smiled to herself as if she were dreaming, as if she were thinking of beautiful nights gone by.

CHAPTER ELEVEN

At the cemetery, Liebling hummed the same melody to himself as he walked alongside the headstones.

He knew that when he first came across Rayne back in 1932 putting together her all-girl jazz ensemble, he challenged her that he could make them the top band in the country.

She bit, and ever since, when she needed a bit of publicity, she gave him a call.

Liebling grinned to himself, feeling his fangs brush sharply up against his lips.

He shut the gate of his crypt and slipped into the shadows.

TO YOUR GRAVE

JENNY COVINGTON

Anna's life never looked like it could fall apart like other people's lives did.

She and Jake, her boyfriend of ten years, lived the perfect DINK lifestyle. Dual income, no kids. Free to use their money as they pleased and live an easy life. They looked like the typical hipster couple. Anna was redhead, long and lithe. She had the build of a gazelle and was one of the best cross country runners during her high school years. Jake had tattoos on both arms and managed a department at Peet's coffee. Making a combined income of over six-figures, they could save. They were considering using their savings to roam the world, then working another ten years and buying a house. Which would sort of make up for Anna's dreary job at the dairy plant. It wasn't anything glamorous, no dairy plant work could realistically be considered glamorous. And it wasn't interesting or exciting either, just the office work that kept the plant in order. Accounts, moving books, telling people when they were too early or late... The only true highlight was her friend, Tina.

And today Tina was late, as usual.

"It's like you don't take your work seriously." Anna sighed. "You're late by a whole hour today. I should be giving you a form to fill in."

"But you won't, cause I'm cute." Tina pulled an exaggerated pout before collapsing into her chair and putting on the kettle. A petite young woman at five-two, she looked up to Anna in more ways than one. Her big brown eyes and ivory skin got her plenty of suitors in the office, even some of the married men couldn't help but ask her out. "Coffee?"

Anna nodded. "Sure, let's have a refill."

"Can't stay mad at me?" Tina laughed as she reached for her favorite flavor, pumpkin, in the cupboard. She scooped out the brownish-orange powder and poured it into two cups of hot water.

"Not when you're making coffee... Besides, it's not like anyone saw you."

"*Thank you.*" Tina muttered in a sing-song voice, stirring the brew.

"I wish I could sound as alert and happy as you."

"Just sleep an extra four or five hours, it'll be fine," Tina laughed.

"If only I had the time..."

Tina shrugged and handed Anna the hot cup. "It's not like you don't make enough money, why not have a break?"

Anna shook her head. "Nah, Jake and I almost have enough for our round the world year. It's taken a bit, but we'll make it."

Tina shook her head. "Ten years of savings to blow in a year." She blew at the steam over her coffee then took a sip. "Mmmmm. I am the best and my coffee is the best."

Anna laughed, it wasn't like little home grown Tina would get it. "Well, we had the plan, save for ten years, travel the world. Save another ten years, get a house. Save another ten years, retire."

Tina nodded. "I guess it gets easier as your salaries go up. But it'll be wrecked when you have kids. My sister has three and they're eating her out of house and home."

Anna scowled. "No kids, no way." Not for her, at least. She wanted to live a freer, happier life than that.

"You say that *now*," Tina said, testing the heat of the coffee again, "but most folks I know are changing their minds already. The baby bug can still get you."

Anna shook her head and smiled. "Not me. I'll get a dog." She laughed a bit and they both settled in for work. No, she wouldn't ever want kids. She was twenty six now, she'd be thirty six when they had a house and forty six when they retired. No time in there to change nappies and run around after babies. Although... "I suppose we might need to spend some money on marriage." Anna added almost wistfully.

"Marriage?" Tina looked up over her computer. "Has Jake proposed?"

Anna shook her head. "No, but he's bound to, isn't he? I mean, we've been together ten years now, since we went to that Summer camp.

We've pretty much followed each other around everywhere. We've lived together for four years. Why not get married?"

Tina shook her head and laughed a bit.

"What's that about?" Anna growled. She never liked it when Tina, home grown, immature, less educated Tina, acted so condescending.

"He just doesn't seem like the type to root down." She replied. "Remember when I first met him?"

Anna nodded. "You said he looked like the polygamous type and said we wouldn't last."

"Well, I still get that vibe from him. He doesn't feel like the sort of guy who'd marry."

"Well, you were wrong about that and you're wrong now. I bet he wants to propose somewhere nice on holiday." Anna retorted.

Tina raised her eyebrows sarcastically and sipped her coffee.

She didn't give it much more thought over the day, but on her way home, Anna felt doubt and anger building up inside her. Sure, Jake never seemed like the monogamous type. Not to her, not to Tina and not to anyone. At camp everyone knew he was the guy who got into tens of teen panties and for some reason most of the girls were proud of it. And he was a disgusting flirt at all times. But their relationship had been on better grounds. Anna had held back for months to make sure he could be loyal to her and Jake seemed willing to work hard for a real relationship with her. She had followed his university choice and later crossed the country to find work in the town where he was hired. Of course he would be loyal to her. He had to be...

But little things were starting to nag at her. The flirting. The late nights. The lack of an engagement, or even a promise ring. She had bought them both promise rings and wore hers religiously. But his rested on his bedside table at all times.

She would start light. As soon as she got home she made a beeline for the bedroom and then for the living room, where Jake sat in his boxers, watching TV.

"Hi sweetie." He said. "Busy day?"

"Mad busy." Anna grinned. "By the way, seeing as we're going abroad in a few months, I'd really, really like you to start wearing this." She handed him the ring.

He looked it over and put it down on the table. "You know I don't do jewellery, sweetie."

"But this is different." Anna insisted. "It's like that necklace you wore for your mother. You **wore** that so she knew you cared about her cause, right?"

"Yeah, but why wear a stupid ring to show I'm your boyfriend?"

"To keep the other girls away, to show you care about me."

Jake laughed. "I *do* care about you Anna... But people wear these if they plan on marrying and, to be honest, I never said I wanted to marry you."

Anna was taken aback, for a few seconds she didn't know what to say and fiddled with her ring. "But, you want to be with me forever, right?"

"Of course, just not married." Jake put the ring down on the table.

"And only me, right?"

Jake fell silent. "I've said I'm not comfortable having this talk." He finally said. This was what he always said when she brought up marriage, commitment or past girlfriends.

"But I just need to know. All you have to say is 'only you sweetie' and I'm good." She shrugged.

Jake shrugged back and continued watching the TV. He was unbelievable. Anna turned and walked into the kitchen to make dinner. How could he be like that? How could he be so stubborn, so non committal. He said he wanted to be with her forever. They had plans for a life together into his fifties. Sure, he didn't have to marry or wear the ring, but she'd like him to at least acknowledge her as his girlfriend, as his life partner. Especially before they went on holiday together. She sighed as she chopped the onions. Did he have to be so difficult?

She heard a knock on the edge of the kitchen door frame. She ignored him.

He walked up behind her and hugged her. "Come on sweetie, don't be like that."

She sighed. "What is it with you and commitment?"

She felt him shrug as he held her. "Do you want me to be honest?"

"Of course, always."

"I've never been a one-chick man. I've never had to commit to one person. And I don't like the idea of promising anyone forever."

"But we're making all these plans together... I get the marriage thing, with divorce stats and all, but..." Anna sighed. It was awkward to put her thoughts into words.

She felt Jake sigh as well. "Anna, I can't promise you commitment. It's not what I do. You've been my only girl most of the time, and always been my main girl, but I can't say there isn't anyone else, that there will never be anyone else or that they're just one night things, I..."

Anna turned in his arms and pushed him back. "You *what*?"

"Sweetie, I figured you knew. I mean, everyone knows, right? My brain likes you and my heart knows you're the one, but my dick, he..."

"Who is she?" Anna asked. She couldn't believe it. He was seeing another girl? "How long?"

"Well, them... pretty much from the start. I mean, you didn't expect me to go for months without, did you? I figured that was what you wanted... you got the relationship, I got the sex."

Anna moved forward and shoved him hard. He fell over on his back. "You're a worthless, lying cunt. I can't believe I trusted you for so long. I can't believe I didn't notice..." She stopped. She couldn't believe she hadn't noticed the look on his face. The blood. She looked down at her hand. The knife was in it, dripping red. The blood pooled under him and around the tear in his belly. His eyes stared blankly at the ceiling. His chest was still.

Anna let out a choked, squeaky gasp and dropped the knife, backing herself up against the counter, trying to get away from that horrible scene. She had killed him. She had killed Jake. She hadn't meant to. But she had.

She looked at the flecks of blood on her hands and, edging her way around the body, ran to the bathroom to wash them. She scrubbed until her skin was grazed and her hands were pink and swollen. She then collapsed next to the sink. What next? What next? Her mind raced. She'd just killed someone. She'd go to jail. No holidays around the world, no home together, nothing. Not to mention that without Jake it would all seem hollow and meaningless...

But for now she had to hide the evidence. Reluctantly looking at her freshly cleaned hands, she gazed out the door. She had to do something. But what? She contemplated a story she read online a few weeks back about a man who killed his wife and, rather than dispose of the body, ate the flesh. But her stomach turned. She couldn't eat Jake. And throwing him in the bin would be obvious. They would probably be able to track him back to her eventually. For now... for now he had to stay in the flat.

Carefully avoiding looking into the kitchen, Anna made her way to the bedroom and dug out a large suitcase. It was the one they had planned on using for their round-the-world trip. They were going to share it. She smiled a little. Oh well, it was all for him now. She threw out the few items in the bottom of it and made her way to the kitchen, half expecting him to be stood there, finishing making dinner. But the onions were still half chopped and Jake still lay there, paler than before, with the knife by his foot. Anna swallowed hard. This would take some doing.

She opened the suitcase on the floor beside Jake and tried to lift him. His cold body was much heavier than she ever remembered him being. Blood smeared down her arms and front. He was too heavy. Too heavy. She dropped him again and he splattered his own blood across the tiles. She resisted the urge to run back to the bathroom for a shower. She looked at the case. The blood would spread through it and ruin it.

She searched through the kitchen drawers for bin bags and carefully lined the case with them, bag after bag, layer after layer, again and again. Satisfied, she looked at Jake. She would start with the legs. They lifted into the bag surprisingly easily, although as she moved his limbs she noticed a wet, brownish pool in the blood and the stench of feces. She had to persevere. Using his knees as a lever, she managed to lift his hip up and into the bag. His lower portions occupied most of it. She carefully rearranged and bent his legs until there was more room. Then she moved to his shoulders and forced his back into the case. She curled him over himself and wedged his arms in as best she could.

Layering more towels and plastic bags over his body, she covered his face last of all before zipping up the case. It would have to stay there for now. It was heavy. She was tired. She glanced at the massive stain on the floor. And she had work to do.

She knew that piles of bloody paper towels in their tiny apartment bin would raise suspicion. So she gathered all but one of the remaining dark towels and a few dark bedsheets and used them to soak the blood up. After half an hour, she passed the last clean bed sheet over the floor. It was sparkling. They were all thrown in the bathtub and she put the shower on full, undressing before throwing her clothes into the pile and stepping in with a bottle of detergent.

Under the scalding hot shower, she scrubbed at each item until the water ran clear off it. Then, she put them into a pile to take to the washing machine. By the end her hands were sore and red again and she could hardly stand, she was so sick, aching and shaky. She wobbled to her feet under the shower head and meticulously scrubbed every inch of her skin clean before stepping out and wrapping herself in the last dark brown towel.

Once the laundry was on she felt much better. She looked from the bathroom to the kitchen and found no specks of blood from the dirty sheets and towels. She checked the kitchen and the sight of the suitcase reassured her. She picked up the knife from the floor and rinsed it under the hot tap before mopping the floor with scalding water from the kettle and making herself a cup of tea with what was left. She nodded to herself as she looked over the kitchen floor, hearing the washing machine hum in the background.

Looking at the clock, she saw it was half past ten already. Where did the time go?

She took her tea with her into the bedroom, roughly dried her hair with the towel, and got into bed. Turning off the light, she curled up tightly on her side of the bed, as far from Jake's side as she could get, and cried herself to sleep.

The next morning she could hardly move. It all felt like a bad dream and she was hoping to roll over and see Jake asleep next to her. But she was scared of not finding him there. Or of finding him there, dead and unmoving. So she lay on her side of the bed, the alarm on her phone screaming at her, louder each time. She could have sworn she felt movement on the other side of the bed and it made her curl up tighter.

As the light between the curtains grew brighter, so did her courage. She rolled over, bracing herself for whatever she might find there... Nothing. The bed was empty besides her. His side was undisturbed. She breathed a sigh of half relief and glanced from her tea, to his empty bedside table, to the time on her still screaming phone. She had fifteen minutes to make it to work on time. Fifteen minutes to check the laundry, the bathroom and the kitchen again, get dressed, grab her things and go to work.

"Come on Anna, we have to get back to normal." She told herself. She stood up and turned her alarm off. She swallowed the bitter, cold tea from her bedside table, down to the lime scaled dregs. *"I'll get dressed and ready first."* She told herself, reaching for her clothes. But of course they were in the laundry. She went to the wardrobe and tried to ignore Jake's coats as she grabbed herself a new dress and blouse. She got

dressed first, then went to the bathroom to brush her teeth, do her hair and put on her make-up. It looked bare. Too bare. Of course it did. All the towels were in the washing machine or the laundry pile. She would have to do more laundry when she got back.

The living room was harder than she'd thought. He had apparently put a game on last night and it was there, still on pause, some character stood there waving a sword in the same motion over and over. The controller rested on the table. The remote on Jake's favourite sofa pillow, which was next to the neat pile of yesterday's work clothes and the not so neat pile of unopened mail. Anna moved to turn the TV off. It was hard. But it felt better once it was done. She walked past the kitchen, not looking in, as she collected her shoes from the hallway and slipped into them.

For a moment she struggled with the choices of going into work without looking at the kitchen, or checking, just to make sure it wasn't all a dream. But it wasn't a dream, and as the image of Jake's corpse folded up in that suitcase brought tears to her eyes, she realized that if she was going to make it through the day she would have to wait to see him again.

She grabbed her handbag and her keys. But she would see him again. Just once more. She would unzip him and look at him once more before she worked out where to bury him.

On the drive into work she felt strangely collected, calm, together. Was it really this easy? She hadn't wanted to, hadn't intended to, but was it really this easy to kill someone? Was she really going to get away with it? In the books they talked about the guilt and that feeling that someone somewhere knew. But nobody knew. There had been no screams, no row. The neighbours would have barely heard them talking. She had raised her voice a bit near the end, but nothing else. And he died so soon when the knife pierced him. She hadn't even screamed after that, she hadn't had the energy.

The people at work would be expecting him. They may call her when he didn't answer his phone. But she could say something... anything. What could she say? He had gone to work? No, that would be too obvious. Someone could easily disprove that, especially as his car was in the drive. She could say they had an argument and he went for a walk. That she had noticed the car was still there and assumed he was staying with a girlfriend. After all, everyone knew he had girlfriends, right?

When she got to work and went to put the kettle on, she saw her hands were, in fact, shaking. When had this started? They weren't like that in the car...

"Good morning Anna."

Anna jumped and turned to see Tina. She must have stared, because Tina looked startled herself.

"What's the matter?" Tina asked.

"You're early." Anna improvised.

Tina burst out laughing. "Can't I be here on time for once?"

Anna shook her head. "No, it's good. Coffee?"

Tina nodded and unpacked her bag. "Why are your hands so shaky?"

"The shock of having someone other than me in here."

"What did you think it was? A ghost?" Tina laughed some more.

Anna froze again. No, of course not... She sighed and tried to steady her hands as she made the coffees.

"Something's different." Tina said as Anna handed her the coffee.

"No, it's the usual blend."

"I mean with you." Tina looked Anna square in the eye.

Anna shrugged, looked to her feet, then back up. She had to come up with something... anything... or at least use the planned argument. What was it? She sighed. "I think Jake left me."

"Oh my God, no." Tina put her coffee down. "How? Why?"

"Well, I asked him to wear the ring, we argued, he said he wanted more freedom in a relationship and he left. Normally he goes for a walk, but he wasn't back this morning. He's probably with that girl." Anna sighed again.

"You'll be fine without him. You two were pretty independent anyway, right?"

Anna nodded. "Yeah, to be honest I'm glad." Was she really glad? That he was gone? Yes. That he was dead? Maybe. No, she couldn't be. She shook her head and sighed again. "I'll manage."

"Attagirl."

The rest of the work day wasn't so bad. Nobody called her from Jake's work in the end. And she didn't have anyone guessing Jake was dead. She just didn't talk about him and felt her hands go shaky now and again. But other than that it was fine. Even the drive home went as usual.

It was on the way up the stairs that she felt nervous again. Like she would open the door and see him staring at the TV screen again in his boxers. She unlocked the door and walked in. The apartment was dark and empty. Impulsively, she put on every light in the house. It felt cold too. She put the heating on before having a look inside the kitchen. The case was still there. Tentatively, she shoved it aside. No marks or stains under it. No blood dripping out of the edges. Just the case resting in the middle of the floor. She couldn't even smell anything. It was a pity to open it back up. But she opened it anyway. She unzipped the case and flung the lid over. The smell hit her hard in the face. It smelled of a butcher's shop in a public rest-room. She looked at the towel that covered his face. She peeled it back.

His skin had lost every drop of colour, even his lips, even his under eye purple bags. It was paler than she had ever seen anyone. Even when people were very ill, they had some blood flow deep under the skin that made them look pinkish or grey. He looked like someone had stretched translucent white silk over something faintly blue and grey. There was no warmth to his colour at all. His hairs looked like they were drawn on his face and head with black marker. His lips had pulled back from his teeth and his eyelids had opened slightly, revealing not just the white, but some of the coloured iris and black pupil as well. His teeth and tongue, faintly visible between the stretched lips, looked bone dry.

Anna retched and ran to the bathroom, flinging herself over the edge of the toilet bowl where she heaved until she brought up yellow bile. Whatever had gone in that day was coming out. She dried her face with some tissue and flushed it. She would have to go back to the case. She would have to cover his face again and zip him up. She drew a deep breath and wandered into the kitchen again. Strangely, the smell was hardly present. She knelt down beside the case and reached for the towel.

"You know, I really wish you wouldn't do that." Jake said.

Anna froze, the towel slipping through her fingers and landing on his face.

"Oh great, more humiliation. As if sitting in a travel case in my own shit wasn't enough." Jake continued. The towel over his face didn't move and the voice wasn't muffled by the fabric.

Anna slowly lifted it off him again.

"That's better." Jake said as his now open eyes were revealed. The face didn't move.

"You're alive? Oh my God, I'm so sorry, I thought I'd killed you." Anna gasped, touching his face. It was ice cold.

"You did. Fucking idiot. Why would you shove someone in the kidneys before checking your hands?"

"I'm sorry, I- I... I'm going mad." Anna said to herself. She dragged the towel over Jake's face again, closed the case and made her way into the living room, where she curled up on the sofa. The silence was blissful, but short.

"You're not going mad, ya know? Well, you are, but you can't leave me here. I mean, I might not be alive, but I'm still your boyfriend.

Unless that whole knife to the guts thing was a breakup." His voice came through as loud and as clear as if he were sitting next to her.

"You're not real." She replied.

"Of course I am. Come back in. Have a look."

"No, *you're* not. The voice. It isn't real." Anna contested.

"I'm here, aren't I? Look, can we have this argument when I'm not sitting in my own shit? This isn't dignified, Anna. At least get me a shower, put me in some nice clothes and swap these plastics out before you lock me away."

She tried to ignore the voice as she made herself a microwave pizza for dinner and as she ate it, watching a soap, but it seemed the voice was louder than anything else she could hear. In the end, she finished half her dinner and went to bed.

"I'm still waiting Anna." The voice came from next to her. She rolled over in bed to face the usual empty space. "No, not in there. But come to think of it, you never did zip up the case..."

Anna gulped. "Leave me alone!"

"Look, I'm just joshing ya, if I could move I'd be in the shower by now. Come on sweetie, lend me a hand."

Anna sighed. "Will you let me sleep if I do?"

"Of course sweetie."

Getting up, she went into the kitchen. Sure enough, the case was unzipped. She zipped it back up and dragged it into the bathroom. She collected some more plastic bags to line the case and a bin bag to throw away the previous wrappings. Then she unzipped and unwrapped him. He was in a mess. The blood was drying and crackling all over him. There were feces all down his legs from where she had thrown his body around. Gross. She tried moving his body, but it proved impossible. His torso sat up in the case and rested against the side of the bath. She would have to get him in from inside the bath. She stripped off and got into the bath, dreading the feel of his cold, dead, stained body against hers. She grabbed him under the armpits and slowly heaved him in, slipping over and over. Once he was laying down in the bath, she put the hot shower head on and hosed his body down, again and again, with hot water until he looked clean enough to use a sponge on.

"Ah, that's better." Jake said. She had almost forgotten why she was going this.

"Please don't speak." She asked.

"Sorry sweetie."

The silence was almost as bad as him talking. She finished washing him down, packed the newly cleaned and dried towels around him to dry him and went to find some clothes. "I feel insane" She muttered as she took his favourite shirt and a pair of jeans into the bathroom.

"You are." Jake replied. "You know, all that time in a case has got me thinking... what about our holiday?"

"What about it?"

"Well, don't we still have the first tickets? Argentina for two?"

"I suppose." She said, struggling to wriggle the corpse into a shirt.

"And that's next month, right?"

"Yeah." Why was she still talking to a corpse? It felt strange. But she couldn't help but answer.

"Are we still going?"

Anna paused. "You're dead."

"But you could bring me. We could go together. Have a great time."

"You're dead." Anna repeated. She awkwardly finished forcing his jeans up and buttoned them before relining the case. It was easier to get him back into confinement when she had something solid to grip onto, though his arms were still awkwardly positioned. She forced them down hard with the case lid. There was a crack.

"Watch it!" Jake complained.

"A deal's a deal. It's bedtime." Anna left the case in the bathroom and went to bed. He left her alone to sleep. But she couldn't drift off.

Perhaps she should go on her trip to Argentina? Just not in a month. Tomorrow. And not for a few days. Forever. She could hop on a plane and disappear. It would be fine. Easy, even. And how would people track her if she actually went on her round the world trip? She could leave Jake here and all. Just pack up and go.

The next morning, she awoke to her alarm and turned it off before the volume went up. Today was a new day. She packed her bags with everything she would need. Four changes of clothes, make-up, hair products, shoes, some nice jewellery, money, passport. She logged online and booked a new ticket. She was pleased that she got a percentage off it for cancelling her old tickets.

"Aren't you forgetting someone?" Jake asked.

"You're back."

"I'll always be here." Jake replied.

Anna felt a chill run down her spine. "Even if I leave the case?"

"Even if you leave the case." He sounded almost smug.

"Can't I get away?"

"Not from me. But we can both get away together. I mean, think about it. I can't cheat on you now, can I? And no money worries for me. Our savings will take you twice as far and you could even retire in some Asian shithole with the money we have. Just bring me with you and we're together forever."

"That sounds convincing." Anna smiled. It did. It really did sound nice.

"Maybe me dying was the best thing to happen to us." Jake insisted.

"Maybe." Anna added extra carry on to her plane ticket.

"When are we leaving?" Jake asked.

"This afternoon. Train down to the airport, then straight to Argentina." Anna replied.

"That sounds awesome."

Anna rang work and told them that she and Jake were back together and heading to Argentina early, that she was quitting and wouldn't be back. There were a few tears, but mostly nobody cared. She called her friends and told them she would Skype as soon as they were there. She rang the landlord and explained she would leave the last month's payment on the table and the keys through the letterbox. She called a taxi and asked the driver to collect her bags.

The driver seemed apprehensive about the smell. Anna could hardly notice it herself, but the man almost gagged when he picked up Jake's case.

Anna shrugged. "I didn't have time to wash the laundry before going. Sorry."

The driver shook his head, dragged the luggage downstairs and threw the case in the back before slamming the boot shut.

"Ouch. Bastard." Jake muttered.

"Soon we'll be in Argentina." Anna smiled as she sat back in the passenger seat.

"We?" The driver asked.

"Uh, I'm meeting some folks there." Anna smiled some more.

"Uh-huh." The driver shook his head again and started the car.

Once they were there and unloaded, the taxi couldn't get away soon enough. He threw the cases down for Anna, got back in and drove off. He even forgot his payment. Anna shrugged. "All the more for us." She started dragging the cases along the station. Even on wheels, Jake weighed so much they wouldn't turn and they were grinding and squeaking as she hauled him across to the right end of the platform. One side faced the rails and on the other was a small wall overlooking an artificial lake. She wondered why it was there and how come there was so little protection between her and the water. It seemed ridiculous.

Looking around at her fellow passengers, they all seemed to be staring at her. She lifted her hand to scratch her head and realized she was still exactly as she had come out of bed. Suddenly she felt self-conscious, but there wasn't anything she could do now. And still, they stared...

She sat down on Jake's case and sighed. Well, at least they wouldn't live here much longer. That way she wouldn't be the weirdo in town. Who cared what these people thought?

But chills travelled down her spine when she spotted the police officer out of the corner of her eye. She knew that the woman with the caramel skin and the blue shirt was looking for her. She had to be. She was glancing up and down, marching decidedly towards that end of the platform. The policewoman *knew*.

"She knows." Jake said. "She knows what you did. She'll find the smell and find me and, well, who would believe you?"

Anna swallowed hard. Only one thing for it. She stood up and looked at the case.

"Anna? What are you doing?" Jake asked, sounding a bit nervous.

Anna began pushing the case towards the wall.

"You're only drawing attention to yourself sweetie." He pressed.

She turned the case on its side by the tiny wall. It would easily flip over.

"Shit, Anna, don't do this. Don't do this to me." The voice grew louder.

Anna glanced down the platform to see the officer start running towards her. She shoved the case into the artificial lake. At first it looked like it would get stuck on the concrete slope. But slowly it slid down, down, down into the water.

"You bitch." Jake said as the officer's hand seized Anna's arm.

"Is everything OK?" The officer asked.

Anna shook. "Yeah." Her eyes met the woman's. The officer wasn't impressed.

"You have to come with me sweetie." She said.

Anna felt repulsed at being called that by anyone but Jake. She stared longingly at the waters that had swallowed his body for good.

In the station, the officer asked Anna a few random questions. Who she was. Where she was going. Why was she going so suddenly. Why hadn't she got dressed in the morning. Anna answered as honestly as possible. She was Anna Mann. She was going to Argentina. She wanted a break. She had been a bit late. Jake's voice was gone and her mind felt so clear, so fresh and invigorated. Officer Terry Welsch nodded, smiled, took notes and went to make a phone call. It was all seeming to look like the officer would write it up to misunderstanding. If Anna could get away before they trenched out Jake's body, then... Then maybe...

"Sorry sweetie." She said, walking into the room. "We can't seem to find your bag."

Anna sighed and groaned. "Great, I'll have to go clothes shopping in Argentina."

"We could *all* do with some clothes shopping." Terry sighed. "Speaking of which, it's warm in here." She undid the very top button of her tight blue shirt, revealing more caramel skin and a necklace. A necklace Anna would have recognized anywhere.

Terry followed Anna's eye-line. "Oh yeah, my boyfriend gave it to me. Said his mother made him wear it for some charity thing. Well, I should say ex boyfriend. Fucker stood me up last night. Sort of like yours." Terry laughed. "I guess I should throw it, only... I don't know, I kinda like it." She shrugged and turned, walking to the door where she started fiddling with the AC. "I swear, it's awful in here. Maybe it's broke again..."

Anna glanced down at the table. The only thing on it was a pen. But she'd seen in a film that a pen, driven through an eye or an ear with enough force, could easily kill...

SHIT HOLE

MARY SAVAGE

Chapter One

He'd spent five years in that hellhole before he made an informed decision: prison fucking sucks. He spent the majority of his day locked in a cell with some psychopath that claimed to hear voices in his head telling him to do crazy shit like wear his underwear on his head or punch that big guy, Stone, in the yard. Stone had nearly killed the poor bastard, but Joe Sullivan, aka "Sully" here, didn't give two shits about him. Not when he ate something gray that might have once been meat for breakfast, lunch, *and* dinner and drank water with a yellowish tint to it. Not when he slept on mattresses lumpier than the alley floors he used to sleep on as a kid, when his mother was jobless and they had no place to call home. Not when he had these assholes who call themselves correctional officers screaming in his ear like they're talking to some old deaf guy and shoving him around like it's some kind of game.

So many times he's wanted to retaliate, to bash their heads in, to slit their throats with a handmade shank, to slap their own cuffs onto their wrists and beat them mercilessly with their own nightsticks. But he was smarter than that; he knew that were he to so much as pluck a single hair from any guard's head, there would be consequences. Namely, more time added on to his sentence and even harsher punishment from the dickheads within the prison itself; the very same ones that were supposed to be protecting him from his other cell mates.

But the very worst part about all of this shit was the fact that he hadn't even done anything wrong to deserve it—well, at least not what they *thought* he'd done.

He's not going to lie; he's wasted a few traitors to the gang. More than one man is buried six feet under with his trademark cigarette burn on the back of the neck, but he swears on his mother's grave that he never even went near that chick they're saying he offed. He didn't even recognize her name, but apparently she was some rich bitch daughter of a senator or something. Raped and killed and dumped in an alley about a mile away from his house, a cigarette burn on the back of her neck and a threatening letter—supposedly from him—found in the pocket of her designer coat.

The police had barely even had to prove his guilt. He was so well-known in this city, by all the jurors and the deliberation had taken less than a minute before he was found Guilty of all crimes. He was sentenced to 20-Life and sent upstream. His girl, Pat, visited him sometimes and they used Morse taps to communicate as they chatted about mundane subjects like the weather and sports games he couldn't give two shits about.

Through their taps, he found out about the man who framed him, Rick Silas, who'd once been his friend, but was now a bitter rival. Rick and Joe had had a falling out years ago over something as absurd as splitting their shares from a lifted purse. There was only about a hundred dollars in the damn thing and Rick's argument was that, since he's the one who distracted the old lady in the first place, he should get a bigger split. Joe fought that it should be equal, since they both did their part in the theft. They'd fought like animals afterwards and one sock in the jaw had Rick backing off.

"Keep it, you greedy fuck!" he roared. "I'll find my own!" It had been a year until he saw Rick again and by that time he already had his own operation going. And Rick was never one to let go of grudges easily.

Cops starting inexplicably hanging around Joe's house, where he, Pat, and their own group of 'outlaws' lived. They sold drugs, stole drugs, used persuasive tactics—such as wielding a knife or a gun—to get their own way, and sold knockoffs. With the cops watching their place, Joe had to be ten times as careful, warding off the fuzz with his natural charm and power of persuasion. He fucked more than one female cop while Pat gave blowjobs to the majority of the males. They weren't bothered at all until the rich bitch turned up dead.

When the cops came to his door then, they didn't even ask questions before shoving a warrant in his face and slapping cuffs on him. At the time, Joe had no idea what he'd done or who had accused him but he already swore revenge as they shoved him into the back of a police car. Nobody wanted to listen to him plead his innocence and his trial was set for the following month, at the senator's insistence.

To find out that it was Rick was no big surprise, but he cursed out loud nonetheless, causing two of the guards to look his way.

"It's supposed to rain tomorrow," he lied and they looked away, uncaring.

It was then that he started to plan his revenge, meeting with Pat every few weeks to tap it out. She informed them that half of their guys had gone over to Rick's side when Joe went away, that they were now loyal to him and they were missing half of their manpower. Nobody had discovered the drug ring, but people were wary about buying from them now that their leader was away. Rick had done all of this, the prick. He would pay.

Now it was five years later and still there was no way to put their plan into action without Joe there to guide them. Pat was persuasive, but she was no gang leader, that was for damn sure. She was just his right hand; the person who echoed his orders and pointed a gun at whoever wavered. She was loyal and tough, but not tough enough for what he had in mind.

He was being driven insane every single day as he listened to his roommate mutter to himself, his head banging a rhythm against the wall. The only thing that kept him going anymore was the thirst for revenge. And Ann's letters.

Ann was another rich bitch. But she hadn't known the victim too well, except for the rumors she heard about the girl's tryst with some gang member. She was the first to write to him and tell him that she believed he was innocent. She wrote, in her first letter, that the gang member the girl was associated with was black, not white like Joe, and lived on the other side of the city—at least according to the rumors she'd heard. She'd tried to tell the cops that but none of them had listened. As far as they were concerned, she was just another little heiress looking for attention.

But the fact that somebody outside his own group thought he was innocent was enough to make Joe respond to that first letter—and then every letter thereafter. Their correspondence lasted for the entirety of his time in prison and he kept every single letter in his pillowcase, smiled when they crinkled at night as he rolled over. He didn't tell Pat about the letters.

He received one on the day his plans would be set into motion.

"Dear Joe,

Since receiving your last letter, I've been thinking a lot about what I would like to do for the rest of my life and I've decided that I'm going to go for it. I'm going to tell my father about my art, show him my paintings. Maybe he'll understand, you know? Maybe he won't be mad at all. I mean, I'm his daughter and he loves me, doesn't he? Won't he just be happy that I'm happy? I'm sure he will and so I'm going to tell him. Better late than never, after all. Right?

And Joe, I don't think I've ever asked you want you want to be. As in your career? I know it'll be a while before you can even consider it, but what is it that you've always wanted to do with your life? Something besides a life of crime, I mean, though to each his own I guess. Let me know in your next letter. I'll be looking forward to it.

Sincerely, Ann Martin"

It was shorter than most of his letters but he tucked it away into the inner coat of his jacket anyway. He would answer no more letters but he wouldn't leave them here, where psycho could get his hands on them. And, besides, having them closer to him made him feel safer as he made his way into the yard, where hundreds of other inmates stood, talking and just taking in the short amount of fresh air they were allotted each day.

Joe strolled casually through the crowds, down a familiar trail, his eyes skating over the faces of guards and his fellow inmates, many of whom were watching him. Platt, a lifer whose cell was located three down from Joe's gave him a hard glance and Joe smirked, held up two fingers, and walked further down the path, approaching the fence. He stopped and sat on the ground, closing his eyes as he counted backwards from a hundred and twenty. At five, his eyes opened again, just in time to see Platt punch Linster in the jaw. This was followed by Brown, another inmate, who sat with Joe at most meals, kneeing some unknown Latino in the groin.

Joe watched as the entire yard dissolved into chaos. The guards all around the yard ran straight towards the mess of inmates fighting one another, throwing punches and kicks and attacking one another with clawed hands. He smiled and reveled in the beauty of it before turning on his head and continuing down the path. Nobody even looked his way.

At the edge of the yard, about a quarter mile away from the entrance into the prison, there was a weak spot of fence. It wasn't electric, for safety reasons, but barbed wire ran all over its length and height—except here. Here, there was a noticeable gap in the barbs, where they split and were easily moved away to reveal a hole in the fence itself. When Joe had first noticed it, after taking a few laps around the sparse yard, there had been no way he could fit through it. It was too small even for the slender Pat to fit through.

But five years, fifty pounds less, and a bit of digging with a hundred or so easily broken plastic spoons, and the hole he made just underneath it might allow him a not-so-easy exit. This was his only chance at escape, either way. He had traded all his belongings to Platt and Brown for their little stunt. Platt didn't take too much convincing but Brown wasn't a lifer and had demanded almost more than Joe could give.

It proved worth it when Joe got down on his knees and slid through the hole like a slithering snake. Maybe he'd lost more weight than he thought in that shithole. He'd have to find a way to make it back after he got settled and wasted that dirtbag of an ex-partner, Rick.

He stood, brushed himself off, and then ran, never looking over his shoulder. The street was just a few hundred yards away and Pat would be waiting for him there, her trunk already open for him to jump into, a bag of fresh clothes for him to change into. She always had him covered, his Pat.

By the time he reached the car, he figured they must be looking for him so he wasted no breath to say hello or thank her for what she was doing. He just jumped into the trunk, shut it, and rolled around as she drove off. But he didn't really care about how sore his muscles were or what a close call he might have just had because he was free.

He was finally fucking free.

Chapter Two

There was absolutely no way they could return to his old house. For one thing, that would have been the first place they looked for him, and for another...well, since his incarceration and the whole operation going belly up and everything, they'd been forced to sell it.

"We got everything out, though," she told him as they walked into the new safe house, located about twenty miles from the city, in the middle of a large wooded area. It had belonged to Pat's late father, used only for fishing and cheating on her mother with his skanks. "It's all here, in the basement. The boys are out on the streets with it right now."

"How do they get back and forth?" Joe asked, always worried about his boys. He tugged his jeans up his hips; they were too big for him now.

"I drive them," Pat told him. "And Jimmy's got a good car now, too."

"Jimmy's sixteen," Joe snorted, looking around the tiny, damp living room.

"Not anymore," Pat said, tugging his hand as she moved towards the couch. "He's got a girl and a kid now. He's got a job down at the docks."

"And he's still selling?"

"He's still loyal. Besides, he ain't making enough to support his family with that dock shit; he needs the cash so I try to help him out, you know." Pat pushed him down onto the couch and climbed up onto his lap, smiling down on him like the Cheshire cat. "Let's not talk about it now, though, alright? We got more important things to do." She began to press kisses against his neck, smiling against his skin as he planted his hands on her hips.

"Pat, babe, we shouldn't—" he started but she pulled back and placed one finger against his lips to silence him.

"We've got plenty of time to do other shit, Joey," she said, "but you've been locked up for half a decade; surely there's something you missed in that time, huh? A bit more, uh, *pressing* issue." She palmed him and he groaned. "See? Now just sit back and relax; Patti's got it all covered, baby."

He was too distracted to argue further.

They lay in bed after three full rounds of what could barely be called sex. It was more like Pat had pounced on him, doing 90% of the work while he just lay there, reaping the benefits. The bed in the master bedroom was ten times as comfortable as the old prison mattress and he found himself starting to drift off as Pat lay against him, catching him up on everything that had happened since their last prison visit.

"...and he got that Martin girl all tied up somewhere in his house. Also, Jimmy's girl is pregnant again with a—"

"Wait," Joe interrupted. "What did you say? About the Martin girl? You mean *Ann*?"

"Yah, I think that's 'er name. Why? You know her?" Pat asked, looking up at him.

Joe nodded as he sat up, dislodging Pat. "Yeah," he said. "she, ah, wrote to me. In prison."

"She's one of *those* chicks?" Pat laughed. "Crazy ass women fallin' for convicts who'd sooner kill them than—"

"You sayin' I'm a murderer, Pat?" Joe barked, startling her.

"'Course not, Joey," she assured him. "I mean, I know you killed people, but those bastards always had it comin', didn't they? So it's all good. I'm just saying *she* didn't know that, is all."

Joe took a deep breath and rubbed the back of his neck. "I know what you're sayin'," he said. "But Ann didn't think I was guilty. She said I must've been framed 'cause I didn't match the description of the girl's boyfriend. Apparently, he was in a gang too."

"Did she say which?" Ann asked, sitting up to rest on her knees next to him.

Joe nodded. "It was Rick's, obviously," he said. "We know that. Poor girl was probably lured in and murdered in cold blood."

"Not before they got their way with her I'll bet," Pat huffed. "Poor...what was her name again?"

"Something Grant, I don't fuckin' know," Joe sighed. "Point is, he killed that poor girl just to get back at me and now he's gonna kill Ann, too. 'Less we do somethin' about it."

"Which we are," Pat reminded him. "In just a few short weeks, we're gonna infiltrate his place and—"

"We don't have weeks, Patti," Joey growled, throwing the sheets off of his legs and standing. He grabbed his boxers and began pulling his clothes on. "We don't even have a few days. You know Rick; he'll play with his new little toy for a few days and then he'll get bored, shoot her dead, and bury her in the backyard." He shook his head. "I've seen him do it too many times and I ain't about to let another girl die on my account."

"So what do you wanna do, then?" Pat asked, following him out of the room, a sheet wrapped around her naked body. "Just storm in there with no backup *tonight*? He's got a million guys in that house of his; ain't no way we're gonna take them all down, just the two of us."

"He won't be keeping her in his house, anyway," Joe dismissed. "He's too smart for that. 'Specially since that girl's daddy is probably lookin' everywhere for her right at this very moment. No, he's keepin' her somewhere, but wh—" His eyes widened as he looked back at Pat. "Is Sabretooth still around?"

"You mean Rick's bitch?" Pat snorted humorlessly, shaking her head, dirty redhead locks shaking with the motion. "'Course he is. But you don't think..." Joe grinned. "Rick wouldn't keep that girl with Sabe; he's a twice-convicted rapist. He couldn't expect the perv to resist somebody like that."

"You said it yourself; Sabretooth is Rick's bitch; whatever he says, that dumbass does. Rick probably distracted him with a couple dozen of his own hoes, anyhow." He paused to take a breath. "Where's he livin' now, Sabretooth. He still got that house on Seventh?"

"Far as I know," Pat said. "I haven't spoken to the bastard in years, but I don't really see any reason for him to change his address; he's been out of jail eight years now. Supposedly, he's doing good, despite more allegations coming up on the contrary." She shook her head. "Even if Sabe *does* have the Martin girl, do you know how hard it's gonna be to bring down all *his* goons? We're gonna need at least a half dozen of our guys and I don't think they'll be up for something like that tonight, babe."

"First light, then," Joe said. "We'll leave when the sun rises; make sure everybody's got their shit together."

"Sweetheart," Pat replied, "I'm loyal to you; you know I am. But I ain't no miracle worker and those boys haven't had their shit together since they was in diapers."

Chapter Three

By morning, all but three of Joe's main group of men had arrived back to Pat's safehouse. Jimmy, Sam, and Teddy were all family men now, which surprised Joe but he wasn't about to take them away from what they'd all worked so hard to gain.

Besides, even without them he still had more than a dozen guys ready to help him take Sabretooth down. Sabe had been one of them once, before Rick had betrayed them all. It hadn't taken the bastard a week to pack up all his shit and run to Rick's side, though. Joe hadn't even been surprised—nor did he care, considering Sabretooth was a lousy shot and proved to be a double-crosser, anyway. Who needed him?

Thankfully, all the men that stayed knew Sabe well enough to know all his tells and his strengths and weaknesses and how fucking dumb that man got when anything in a skirt showed up. He thought with his dick and that was a fatal flaw that made Joe burst into random bouts of laughter. His boys followed.

The plan was simple: Their three strongest—Bo, Gabe, and Devon—would lead the group. Being the muscle meant that they'd be able to easily take out any shitheads guarding around the house and allow the rest to get in. Behind them were about six of Joe's most weapon-savvy men; TJ, Mart, Steve, Bardy, Paulie, and Fisher. Their weapons were, for the most part, concealed by their clothing, but easily accessible when they needed them. They would enter the house before Pat, Joe, and the rest, guns blazing as they took out anyone on the first floor (though they were warned to be way of any redhead girls who looked as if they might be scared or mistreated.) Once they cleared, Joe and Pat would lead the others upstairs, where Ann was most likely be held. He knew, from experience, that there were only three possible rooms she could be held in, so they would be split into partners. He and Pat would be together, of course.

"This girl really that important to you?" Dove, the only other female gang member asked as they waited for the all-clear from Bardy. "I wouldn't even go that far for a piece of ass."

"She ain't a piece of ass, Dove," Joe snapped. "She's an innocent. And the only person who believed me when she didn't have to. We don't let people like that die on our watch, alright?"

"Okay, okay," Dove muttered. "Damn."

"Clear!" Bardy called out to Joe and he lead them out from the gathering of bushes they'd been hiding in, each pulling out their weapons as they approached the house. Joe took the safety off his Glock as he immediately started up the stairs. Pat was on his heel. At the top of the stairs, they split into their groups. Dove went with Stu, and Bardy would search another room with TJ, while Pat and Joe took the last room.

"You ready for this?" Pat asked him. "You might not like what you see. She might already be dead."

"I'll hate myself if I don't make sure," Joe responded. "So, yes. I'm ready."

"Fingers crossed." Pat kicked in the door, her gun pointed inside.

The room was completely empty, but for a few chairs and boxes, and three people. The first was the man himself; Sabretooth was a slimy man with a shark's tooth necklace around his neck. He was skinny and tall and his breath constantly stank of onions. It was no wonder he had to stoop as low as rape to get any action. Just the very sight of him made Joe's stomach lurch; he was sickening.

Behind him was a scantily clad, brown-skinned woman with firetruck-red short hair that hung over her eyes in a fringe. She barely even glanced their way, too distracted by the tiny redhead she had her arms wrapped around, her lips attached to the pulse point of a visibly uncomfortable young woman.

Ann. That was Joe's Ann. The same woman who's scrawling cursive he'd read at least twice a week since he was sent away. Her dress was torn and her makeup was smudged and her hair looked like a rat's nest, but there was no mistaking the woman in all the pictures she'd sent him over the years. Only the woman in the pictures was constantly smiling; there was no trace of a smile on her face her. Not even when he could clearly read the look recognition on her face. Instead, he looked absolutely terrified.

"What did you do to her?" Joe barked at Sabe, who just grinned in return.

"Hey to you, too, Joey; how've you been?" he responded. "How was prison?"

"What did you do to her?" Joe repeated, completely ignoring the other man's questions.

"Me?" Sabe asked, as if offended. "Absolutely nothing. My girl, Lourdes, however..."

"GET YOUR HANDS OFF OF HER!" Joe boomed, his gun pointing in the woman's direction. She didn't even blink.

"Don't be ridiculous," Sabretooth laughed. "She knows you won't do anything while she'd wrapped around your girl. Lourdes may be a hoe, but she ain't stupid." He laughed again and pulled his own gun. "I, however, don't care about either bitch." He pointed his gun at them and finally Lourdes stopped, her eyes going wide.

"Sabe?" she asked, stepping away from Ann, who fell to the floor in a fit of sobs. Sabretooth wasted no time in shooting her through the school. Lourdes's body fell to the floor as blood gushed from the wound in her head and Ann screamed. Sabretooth pointed the gun at her next and she began to beg and plead for her life.

"He won't hurt you," Joe told her. "He can't."

"The fuck you mean, I can't?" Sabretooth hissed, his gun trained on Ann's head. "You've seen me shoot bitches before, haven't you? Or have you forgotten?"

"I haven't forgotten what a little bitch you are," Joe said, taking a step forward. Sabe's gun swung around to point at him.

"The fuck you say to me?" he growled. "I ain't no bitch."

Joe scoffed. "Of course you are," he said. "You were my bitch for years and then you left me to be Rick's bitch. And no bitch of Rick's is about to kill his favorite toy; not if he don't wanna be killed in return. Trust me, Sabe, you're a total bitch."

"You wanna see a bitch, motherfucker?" Sabretooth growled. "Why do you watch me waste *yours*?" His head started to swing back but before it could, Ann's hand slapped down on it, forcing the gun out of his grip. It clattered across the floor and she immediately jumped after it. So did Sabretooth, but before he could pull the redhead back, Pat shot his leg and he cried out in pain. "BITCH!" he bellowed.

"You know it," Pat replied, blowing on the muzzle of her gun, before re-holstering it. Ann was able to grab the gun and stood, pointing it down at Sabretooth, who was immobilized by the pain in his leg but looked up at the shaky weapon with defiance.

"What are you gonna do, bitch?" he asked. "Shoot me? You don't got the balls."

Ann glared at him but her hands continued to shake. She took a step back and Sabe laughed. Pat shook her head and glanced up at Joe. "You want me to waste him?" she asked.

"No," Joe said, his eyes trained on Ann. "Let her do it." Ann looked up at that and her eyes pleaded with him. She shook her head. "It's alright," he said. "Think about all the horrible things he did to you. Think about what he did to Lourdes, his own girl. He was about to do the same to you. He deserves this, alright? Nobody would blame you for offin' him. And, trust me, it feels so fuckin' good to do an asshole like that in, to give him what he deserves. Just go ahead and you'll see. Trust me, Ann. Do you trust me?" Ann nodded, but continued to waver. "You'll be okay."

She nodded again and pulled the trigger. The sound the gun made was deafening in the silence of the room. Sabretooth's body went limp after the bullet lodged in his cranium and blood splattered over the floor and Ann's bare feet. The gun dropped from her shaky hand to the ground and her knees began to wobble. She looked to Joe for help and he stepped forward, catching her in his arms before she could reach the floor.

"I've got you," he whispered against her hair. "I've got you, Ann." She buried her face into his chest and began to sob as he rubbed her back.

Pat watched with undisguised hurt, but Joe didn't notice. She took a deep breath and swallowed past the lump in her throat, turning to the other men. "Come on," she said, "we don't wanna be around when the fuzz shows up." She stormed past the confused group, not even sparing Joe and Ann a glance over her shoulder to see that he'd lifted the woman into his arms and was now carrying her, bridal-style, out of the room.

Joe's eyes remained focused on Ann the whole time. "I'm gonna get you outta here, okay?" he whispered in her ear. "You'll be okay. Gonna get you somewhere nice and safe, alright?"

"Okay," Ann sniffed against his shirt, her arms tight around his neck already.

It was in that moment that Ann Martin realized how deeply and fathomlessly in love she was with Joe Sullivan.

Chapter Four

It took them less than 24 hours to get Ann cleaned up, patched up, buy her some new clothes, feed her, and purchase her a train ticket to Stamford, CT. Her family lived in Manhattan, but Joe figured it would be too easy for anybody to snatch her here in the city. At least in Connecticut she would be safe with Pat's cousin, Carly.

"Now, listen," he told her once they made it to Grand Central, "Carly's gonna meet you at the platform. Don't be stupid and go wandering off alone, okay? Somebody might come after you and you don't want to be alone when that happens. Carly's tough and protective as all hell; she's the one that's gonna keep you safe in our absence."

"But, Joe, I—" Ann started to argue.

"No," Joe cut her off, shaking his head. "No arguments right now, okay? We're trying to save your life and this is the best way to do it, okay?" Ann nodded, tears in her eyes. "Okay. Now, as soon as we've got everything settled over here, either me or Pat is gonna come get you in Stamford. We'll call Carly first to let you know we're on our way, okay?" Ann nodded and Joe gave her a gentle smile. "You're gonna be okay, kid," he said, cupping her cheek with one hand. "Everything's gonna be okay now." Ann took a deep breath and canted into him, wrapping her arms around his neck and pressing her face into his neck.

"Don't die," she whispered, on a shuddery breath. She pulled back. "Promise me you won't die." Her gaze was steely and Joe couldn't help but nod at that.

"I promise," he said and she smiled sadly up at him, leaning up on her toes to press her lips against his. Joe returned her kiss, his hands cupping her slender hips. Pat watched from the side with a frown, before looking away.

"Better wrap it up," she said, suddenly, looking at her watch. "The train is leaving in about ten minutes." Joe and Ann pulled apart, sighing. Tears streamed down Ann's cheeks and Joe brushed them away with his thumbs.

"Everything will be alright," he said again. "You'll see. Now, go." He backed away from her and Ann took a deep breath, grabbing her bag and heading in the direction of her platform. Before she reached it, she looked back and locked eyes with Joe. She gave him one last wave and blew him a kiss and he offered her a weak smile in return.

When she was gone, Joe's smile disappeared and he turned to Pat. "Let's go get this asshole," he practically growled, starting towards the exit. Pat was right on his heels.

Infiltrating Rick's brownstone was a much harder feet than they'd originally thought. He lived on a more populated street, so the outdoor guards were not an option. That was good in some ways, Joe thought, but now they had no idea exactly how many people were actually *inside* the damn building because every single window was blocked by thick curtains. And in the daytime, there would be no lights on to give even a shadow so they were going in completely blind.

"Listen," Joe said as they planned it all out. "We may lose a few good men today. But I want you all to know how glad I am to have you all on my side. You've remained loyal to me for all these years and I'm grateful for that. Each one of you has a place in my heart."

"Did prison turn you into a sap, Sullivan?" Bardy growled out, making the others laugh. "'Cause I thought it was supposed to make you tougher."

"Looks like it had the opposite effect," TJ piped in, making them all laugh again.

"Fuck you all," Joe laughed, shaking his head. "Alright," he said, "let's get on with it. If anybody finds that bastard before me, keep him alive; I wanna be the one to put that bullet through his skull, got it?" They nodded and broke apart.

Trying to appear inconspicuous, they split into groups, their weapons concealed by clothing and bags. Dove and Pat linked arms like girlfriends and pretended to gossip about their boyfriends, strutting down the street in tight dresses and heels. One group of their men pretended to whistle at them as they passed; another group was dressed as businessmen and carried their weapons in briefcases. Joe had on a hoodie and a pair of headphones in his ears that weren't actually connected to anything. Nobody noticed that they were headed in the exact same direction.

There was an alley in between Rick's brownstone and the one next to it, which they all slipped into, one group at a time. From there, Joe was able to get a good look at the back of the building, through the slats of a broken fence. "There's a fire escape leading into the yard," he told Pat. "We could probably climb it while the others start from the first floor; corner him, ya know?"

Pat nodded. "Good plan," she said. "But there's one leading out the front, too."

"You take one," Joe said, "I'll take the other." It wasn't too complicated.

"What if he's not alone?"

Joe groaned. "TJ, go with Pat; Bardy, come with me." The men nodded. "All the rest, start from the bottom and make your way up. From the looks of it, we've got three floors to deal with here. Make sure Rick gets to the third floor and, remember, don't kill the bastard. I'll handle that part."

There were murmurs of agreement as everybody got into position. Pat and TJ went around the front and climbed up the fire escape, careful not to pass clear in front of a window, lest they give themselves away. Nobody from the street even glanced their way.

Joe and Bardy situated themselves on the back fire escape while the rest of their team waited at every possible entrance for a sign from them to begin.

"Everybody in position?" Joe whispered in his walkie talkie. There was a static of yeses coming from each individual talkie and he took a deep breath. "Okay. Go!" The sound of windows breaking, doors slamming open, shouts and growls and gunfire coming from inside. Joe and Bardy waited for the signal from Dove, telling them that it was safe to enter.

Ann Martin didn't get on the train. She couldn't. Not when she knew that Joe's life was in danger; not when she just recently realized how she felt about him. She just couldn't do it.

So she stood on the platform for fifteen minutes, waved stupidly to the train as it pulled out of the station, and then walked off the platform. She was almost relieved to see that Joe and Pat were no longer standing in the middle of Grand Central when she arrived, surrounded by a thousand other people desperately trying to find their own platforms. Tourists took pictures of the big clock and the constellations painted on the ceilings. They took in everything with wide eyes and even wider mouths, like this train station was something exceedingly special.

Ann had lived here for the whole of her life and she knew that there was absolutely nothing special about this place once you've seen for the hundredth time. Her parents had taken her through here so many times on their way to and from Westchester County, where they had an estate in Purchase, that it wore off by the time she was five. The train station, which had once been a colorful world full of excitement and adventure for a toddler, was now just...loud.

Ann hastened towards the exit as quickly as possible and breathed in the stale New York City air with reverence. She'd almost died just one day before and she never felt so grateful for the chance to breath in the smoky, polluted air of the city, to hear the thundering stutters of construction just down the street. To experience the hateful scowl on a native's face as they bumped into her on the sidewalk. She felt as if she were experiencing New York for the very first time.

Dragging her rolling suitcase behind her, she started in the direction of Washington Square Park. It would take her a while to get there, she knew that, but maybe she could...

Ann paused. What could she do? She didn't have any guns and she knew nothing she could say to Joe would help. He was intent on his revenge, intent on killing another man no matter what the consequences, and she knew that. Knew that he wouldn't stop until he achieved his goal. He would gladly go back to prison if it meant Rick Silas was dead on the ground.

But Ann couldn't let that happen. She couldn't lose him again, not like this. And any other way than Joe killing Rick meant that Rick killed Joe and she couldn't live with that knowledge either. So, no matter how long the distance, or how high the stakes, Ann would have to go after her love. She had to stop him, even if she risked her own life in the process.

He was completely worth it. At least in her mind. She just hoped that she wasn't too late.

"We lost Paulie!" Fisher's voice crackled through the walkie. Joe cursed and shared a look with Bardy, who'd practically been Paulie's guardian since the day he joined, a gangly kid of about 15, desperate to prove himself. Bardy had made him the weapons master he was now. Or had been.

"Sorry, man," Joe whispered. Bardy shook his head, his eyes filled with undisguised rage.

"He's gonna fuckin' pay for that," he growled in a low voice. Joe nodded, solemnly. His walkie crackled again.

"WE'VE GOT HIM!" Mart shouted through the line. "He's headed toward the third floor. Patti! Joey! Do you read me?!"

"Got it!" Pat's voice called and Joe could hear her without the damn talkie. "I'm goin' in!"

"Me too," Joe growled into the machine as he and Bardy readied their guns and stepped up to the window. "

"You ready for this?" Bardy asked in his low, rumbling voice.

Joe nodded. "As I'll ever be," he replied, taking a deep breath. Bardy nodded in return and they both turned to face the window. Joe held up one hand and started a slow countdown on it.

Three....two.....one!

They burst through the window, spilling glass into the room with them. They stumbled slightly at their entrance, but then held their guns up high, pointing them around the room.

It was small and crowded with bedroom furniture; a bed, a chest of drawers, an old vanity table and matching wooden bookcase. The window was next to the door and in the next second a familiar face appeared in the doorway, his hands held up over his head, a smug smile on his face.

"Rick Silas," Joe growled, then spit at the man's feet as they walked past. "Long time, no see."

Rick's head turned in their direction, hands staying up as Pat entered the room after him, her gun pointed at Rick's head. He smirked at the sight of his old foe. "Joseph Sullivan," he greeted. "I thought you were locked up."

"Got out early," Joe replied, his teeth gritted. "Good behavior and all that."

Rick snorted. "Good behavior? You?" He laughed a big, honking laugh. "Right. Ain't nobody gonna get out of jail for 'good behavior' when a senator's daughter gets off; least of all, you." He shook his head. "So how's you get out then?"

"Not really important," Joe replied, his gun still raised. "I'm out now, ain't I? Why dwell on the past?"

"Joey Sullivan," Rick sighed, "always thinking of the future; almost as much as you think of yourself, you greedy bastard."

"At least I'm not some whiny little bitch," Joe said. "So focused on getting my revenge that I put the lives of others at risk."

"That isn't what you're doing right now?" Rick retorted, his eyes skating over the injured men and women behind Joe's back.

"These are all *willing* participants," Joe informed him. "I didn't kill an innocent just to make a point. I'm no pussy when it comes to revenge, Silas. Not like you."

"Nobody's innocent," Rick said, smartly, his hands finally lowering. "You taught me that." He reached for his pocket and they all took a step forward. He put one hand back up. "Relax," he said, pulling out a butane lighter. He flicked it open, then closed. "Nervous habit," he explained, calmly, that smirk never leaving his face. Joe watched him calculatingly, before his eyes began to roam around the room.

For the first time since they burst in, he realized why there had been such opaque curtains hanging in every single window. On every surface, including the floor itself, there were candles; most lit, but some blown out, though wisps of smoke still rose from their wicks as if they'd been lit recently. It was no surprise, really, considering that Rick was a pyromaniac. He always had a lighter handy and enjoyed watching the wax melt on his candles. His weapon of choice was an impromptu flamethrower made from a can of hairspray and whatever lighter he typically had handy at the given moment.

His favorite had a picture of the Tasmanian Devil on it. More than once, Joe had joked that Taz was like the animated incarnation of Rick himself; crazy and unpredictable and incredibly volatile. Rick apparently still favored the character as Joe could just make out the little brown blob on the otherwise silver piece of metal. Some things never changed, he thought, as he continued to glare at the other man.

"I can't believe you still have that damn thing," Joe said, surprising himself even. He hadn't meant to start a conversation.

"My loyalty to Taz hasn't changed," Rick replied, still flicking the lid of his lighter open and close.

"At least you remained loyal to him," Joe retorted on a growl. "At least you remained loyal to *somebody.*"

"Still sore about that, are you?" Rick asked, grinning. "I wish you'd just let it go, man. We weren't *that* close."

"I couldn't give a shit less about your little betrayal," Joe informed him. "But what you did *after* that; killing that girl, sending me to prison to *rot* for five fucking years...you had it coming."

"Had what coming?" Rick asked, still smiling as if he didn't know. Joe cocked his gun in response and Rick's grin widened. "Oh," he said. "That." He took a calm breath and shook his head. "You're not *really* going to kill your best chance at going free, are you?" He flicked the lighter open. "The only person who can confirm that you didn't kill that poor Grant girl." He flicked it closed. "Think about it, Joey; if I'm gone, you're just going to go back to prison." Open.

"Not necessarily," Joe countered.

"What else then? You gonna go on the run?" He tilted his head, his eyes shining with amusement. "With your girl, Pat?" Joe's gun wavered and his mouth tightened. "No..." Rick continued with a titter. "That Martin girl? What's her name?" Joe refused to answer but his hand tightened around the gun. "Ann, right?" Joe still did not respond; he didn't have to. "Ann," Rick decided. "How is she? Still smarting from making her first kill?" Joe's eyes widened.

"How did you know about that?" he barked. Rick didn't even blink.

"You still think I don't have eyes everywhere, don't you?" Rick tutted. "Joey, Joey, Joey...when are you gonna learn? I see *everything*," he whispered, his grin becoming catlike.

"See this, punk!" Pat cried as she took a shot. Joe, at the last minute, shoved her arm, causing her bullet to fly at the hand holding Rick's lighter, which dropped on impulse as the man cursed.

"Fucking bitch!" he screamed as he held his hand to his chest. It was bleeding profusely. Joe glared at Pat.

"What did I fucking say?" he growled. She had the decency to look ashamed.

"Sorry," she grumbled. When he turned back to Rick, he was still holding his bleeding hand. And still cursing. "But he deserved it."

"That don't fucking matter," Joe growled at her. "You don't fucking dis—"

"FIRE!" Bardy screamed from behind them. Pat and Joe looked in the direction he was pointing and did, in fact, see a fire begin to bloom from the curtain, where Rick's lit lighter had fallen.

"Shit!" Joe barked, alerting Rick, who turned and let out a string of curses, starting in the direction of the door. Nearly a dozen weapons rose automatically, pointed straight at his head. He paused, turned and ran for the window—the one without the fire escape. He threw aside the curtain and jumped out while everybody watched in shock.

"Did he just fuckin'—" Pat asked.

"Yes," Bardy growled. "Yes, he did."

Joe wasn't convinced. He ran to the window, even as the flames grew around him.

"Joey!" Pat cried. "What the fuck are you doing? We gotta get outta this fuckin' place before it burns to the ground!"

"Go on!" Joe yelled back. "I need to make sure this sonofabitch is dead! I'll take the fire escape."

The others began to run out, some taking the fire escape while other hightailed it down the stairs. "I ain't leavin' you!" Pat cried, even as Dove started to pull her out. Bardy was urging her towards the fire escape, but she wouldn't go.

Joe ignored her, looking out the window. A sadistic grin spread over his features as he spotted Rick's crumpled body in the grass, joints bent at odd angles. He winced once in sympathy and shook his head, backing away from the window.

The room was now engulfed in flames. Those who had rushed to escape had inadvertently knocked over several candles, which only added to the overall fire. The breathable air was diminishing. Pat still stood at the window, hesitant to leave without him. Bardy was tugging on her arm, trying to get her to leave. She refused, pleading with Joe.

He nodded and started after her, before doubling back. He found the lighter next to the lit up curtains and grabbed it: his trophy. He closed it and tucked it deep into his pocket, before turning on his heel and running towards the fire escape.

He'd barely made it with the curtains of those windows burst into flames too, forcing him back. Pat jumped back as well and Bardy attempted to pick her up, but she struggled too much for him to get a good grip.

"We have to go!" he yelled.

"No!" Pat fought. "I won't leave without him!"

"Pat, go!" Joe ordered. "Get out of here!"

"No!" Pat screamed. "Not until I know you're safe!"

"I've got a plan," Joe called back, before turning and running straight to the other window. He took a deep breath before he took a flying leap straight out of it.

"JOE!" Pat screamed just as Bardy got a good hold of her and carried her down the steps.

Joe had jumped out of windows before, but never on the third floor—not when there wasn't a pool below or something else to break his fall. He'd read somewhere that you could lessen the impact by rolling in midair. Well, whoever said that was apparently an idiot who'd never jumped out of a window in their life.

He rolled as soon as he felt himself fly the air—a front flip that would make any amateur gymnast proud—but it did nothing to numb the impact of the ground as he hit it. If anything, it made the fall worse, more painful. Joe could hear the sickening sound of the bones in his legs cracking as he reached the ground. His spine tingled as if pins and needles were stuck all along it, and the pain as his head connected with the ground was like nothing he'd ever felt before. He saw stars appear in front of his eyes. The entire world went silent for a long moment and he thought he died.

He closed his eyes, welcoming it. He'd done what he'd come here to accomplish. The result was lying about a foot away, in worse shape than him, no doubt. He attempted to turn his head but everything hurt and even with his eyes closed he felt his world spinning on its access. So he just lay there, waiting for death to claim him.

As he waited, a ringing started in his ears, muffled crying rising over it. He started to slowly come back to the world, his eyes creaking open, the world blurried until he blinked a couple times and then...

"Ann?" Joe croaked. "Ann, what—?"

"No," Ann whimpered, placing a finger over his lips. "Don't speak, Joe. You're going to be alright, okay? There's an ambulance on the way; they said not to move you." Joe tried to not but that caused even more pain so he settled for breathing. Ann sniffled. "Oh Joe," she sighed. "Joe, you can't leave me. Not now. I need you, baby. You need to hold out; just a little longer."

"Can't," Joe croaked. "Dying."

"No!" Ann cried. "No, you're not; don't say that."

"But, I-I am," he replied. "And th-that's okay."

"No, it's not!" Ann sobbed. "Don't say that! Please don't say that!" Joe shut his eyes and took a breath. When he opened them again, Pat was there. He turned to look at her.

"Pat," he sighed. "Take...take care of her for me, will ya?"

"Don't talk like that, Joey," Pat sniffled. "You're gonna be just fine, alright? Just fine."

"No," Joe sighed. "I'm not. And if...when I'm not here to protect her...you've gotta...okay? Promise me."

"Joe, I—"

"*Promise*," Joe growled.

Pat took a shuddering breath. "Okay," she said. "I promise."

"Good," Joe breathed, turning his eyes back to Ann.

"She'll take good care of you, okay?" he said. Ann nodded, tearfully.

"So will you," she insisted. "You promised. You promised everything would be alright."

Joe sighed. "I'm sorry," he said. "I don't think I'm...I'm going to be able to..." he trailed off and took another breath. "I'm sorry," he said, closing his eyes. After a long, tense moment, they opened again. "Ann," he breathed. "I...I have to tell you something."

"What?" Ann asked, leaning down again. His voice was becoming faint.

"I...I loved you," Joe breathed out, before his eyes shut permanently and his body went completely limp.

Both Pat and Ann dissolved into tears, the former holding the latter as Ann held on to Joe's body, their tears mingling as they fell to his chest. Above their wails, ambulance sirens could be heard.

THE END

TWO KILLERS & A HOOKER

JAKE MICHAELS

111

CHAPTER ONE

Jesse James Hewitt never knew when the killings would come.

All he knew was that violence was the only tool he had.

He wasn't like other serial killers who stalked their victims and preplanned their attacks. Jesse's victims were random, in all shapes, sizes and colors.

That is how he stayed under the radar.

But his hair trigger temper could go off at any time. Right now, as he parked the stolen Toyota Camry in front of the corner grocery store, he felt happy. He had a little money in his pocket and for the next week had a place to stay at his uncle's pad.

Jesse James did, in fact, look like a modern Jesse James. He wore flared out jeans with a leather vest over a blue denim shirt. He ditched the skin head look years ago and instead grew his hair out long, a tousled mop of brown curls that he rarely combed. He had ice blue eyes that charmed many a woman until they got to know the man behind the eyes and soon felt repulsed.

Jesse walked into the store and noticed the young Asian kid leafing through the latest X-men in front of the comic rack.

He approached the young man, startling him as he craned his neck to look at his comic book cover.

"Wolverine and Kitty Pryde!" Jesse said. "Yeah, I'd fuck her."

Walking through the store, Jesse whistled in tune with the Taylor Swift swing that played on the overhead radio. Bored, he picked up a loaf of Wonderbread off the shelf then tossed it aside. Heading toward the beverage aisle, he reached inside the glass and picked up a bottle of his favorite drink.

Chocolate Yoo-Hoo.

He ripped off the lid and guzzled the contents down, the chocolate milk dripping off the side of his mouth.

Belching loud, he drifted over to the second of the three store aisles, grabbing a box of chocolate donuts. His thick fingers ripped through the plastic, breaking off a piece of a donut.

Jesse looked out at the store front window as a police car sped down the street, sirens blaring. Another squad car followed, then another.

"Uh oh," Jesse cried out. "The natives are restless."

Jesse tossed a chunk of the chocolate donut into his mouth before placing the box on the cashier's counter. An Ethiopian girl, no more than twenty years old, gave him a courtesy smile which quickly disappeared. She had caramel-colored skin and had dyed her hair redhead, leaving the tips dark brown. Her name tag read 'Naomi'.

"Hi," Jesse said.

"You find everything okay?" she asked.

"Definitely," he said, eyeballing the slim young woman up and down. "Anybody ever tell you that you look like Jessica Alba?"

"Who?"

"You know, the actress. Full lips. Beautiful face. If she were black, you'd look just like her. Or maybe she'd look just like you."

"I don't know who you're talking about," Naomi said.

"That's charming," he said. "Where are you from?"

"Ethiopia."

"I would have guessed Eritrea," he said, guzzling down the Yoo-Hoo.

"I need to scan it," she said, holding her hand out.

"Oh right," he said, handing the bottle to the young woman.

"Do you like your job?"

"Will this be all, sir?" Naomi asked, ignoring his question.

"No," Jesse said. "You're a beautiful girl and I'm really interested in how you got here and where you're going. What time do you get off?"

"When do I get off?"

"As often as you can, right?" Jesse laughed loud.

Naomi rolled her eyes.

He looked back at the storefront window. "Open twenty-four seven. How about you? Are you open twenty-four seven?"

"Is this your best game?"

"You couldn't handle my game with a referee and a whistle."

Naomi punched buttons on the cash register. "That will be five dollars."

"Think about it," he said. "You. Me. A glass of scotch in front of a warm fire."

"I don't think so."

"Can you look me in the eye when you say that?"

Naomi complied with his request, her facial expression annoyed. "I'll say this real slow so that you can understand. I. Don't. Think. So."

"I have to take you out," Jesse said. "Sometimes, you meet a person and you just know, do you know what I mean, baby?"

"Five dollars, asshole."

"Asshole," Jesse said, his eyes flickering from lust to hatred. "Is that what I am?"

"Sometimes you meet a person and you just know, do you know what I mean?"

"I just hate it," Jesse said, pulling out his gun. "When people come to this country."

He fired into the girl's stomach.

"And they don't see that I'm a local boy that made good."

Jesse grabbed his box of donuts and headed out of the store, leaving Naomi writhing in pain on the floor. The Asian boy dropped the comic and cowered in fear.

Jesse sneered at the young man then feinted as if he were about to shoot him.

"Boo!"

The Asian kid bolted out of the store, running across the street and into traffic. Horns blared.

"Run!" Jesse laughed, blowing the coils of smoke away from his gun. "Run, China Boy, Run!"

CHAPTER TWO

Kelly had walked up and down the liquor aisle for over a half-hour now. Usually, there would be someone in his face asking if he needed help. But this storekeeper seemed content to watch the television up on the corner wall. An obese woman with tinted eyeglasses she stared up at the television screen oblivious to her surroundings.

Kelly knew the feeling. He felt like everything around him was television and that he was an uncredited player in the script. His emotions felt as if they were trapped in quicksand, his tumultuous childhood traumatizing his brain into an endless loop of bad memories.

A permanent nightmare.

Kelly thought he looked inconspicuous. He wore a Golden State Warriors baseball cap and a long black trench coat two sizes too big. Wire-rimmed glasses covered his face which he always kept downcast, giving him the look of a schoolyard pervert. Underweight and undersized, Kelly cultivated the creepy look. It kept people away from him.

"I can't do it," he muttered. "I can't fucking do it."

He went up and down the aisle again but this time he grabbed the bottle of 'two buck Chuck' and hid it inside his trench coat.

"You can do it," he hissed. "Just fucking do it."

He turned down the aisle again.

"No, I can't," Kelly placed the bottle back on the shelf.

"What the fuck are you doing?" Jesse asked, blocking the path of the young man.

"Excuse me?"

"You don't want the booze?"

"No, sir."

"What's wrong with it."

"I'm trying to give it up."

"Everybody's trying to give something up," Jesse said, taking the bottle of Two Buck Chuck back off the shelf. "That's why everybody is so damn miserable. You gotta do the things you love!"

Kelly looked over at the cashier who sat oblivious to their conversation. He saw that her name tag read 'Rosie'.

"See this?" Jesse asked, holding up the bottle of Chocolate Yoo-hoo. "My dentist says I have to stop drinking these. Causes a bunch of cavities. And heart disease. But I can't stop myself. Tastes too damn good. Want to try?"

Kelly shook his head.

Jesse took another swig of his chocolate then eyeballed the wine bottle. "2014. Vintage! You like the old stuff?"

"Yes, sir."

Jesse popped open the cork. "Here," he said, extending the bottle to Kelly. "Try it."

Kelly looked away, a nervous tic in his neck.

"What's wrong? Cat got your tongue?"

"No, sir."

"You got issues," Jesse said, watching Kelly twitch as he started to back down the aisle.

"What's wrong now?" Jesse asked.

Kelly backed into a Mexican woman with a cart full of six packs. She looked to be nine months pregnant.

"Damn, *mamacita*," Jesse said as the woman walked by. "Way to start the kid off right."

"*Chinga tu madre*," the woman said.

"*Adios, amiga*," Jesse rolled his eyes, walking toward Kelly. "You see, that is what I'm talking about. Poor kid has a mother that is boozing it up and he isn't even out of the womb yet. He's got no chance, that kid. Starting off life behind the eight-ball with a mother like that, right?"

Kelly nodded his head in agreement.

"Come on," Jesse said, motioning Kelly to follow him. "You're a cool dude. Good listener. Sometimes you look at somebody and you just know, you know what I mean?"

The two stepped over to the cashier who never took her eye off the television. A game of Jeopardy was on.

Jesse handed the woman a $20 bill for the $15 bottle.

"Here you are, ma'am," he said. "Keep the change."

The cashier rolled her eyes.

"I think you and I are on the same frequency," Jesse said, leading Kelly out of the store. "Are you from the Bay Area?"

"No sir," Kelly said.

"Well, we don't have that in common. But that's okay."

He handed the bottle of wine to Kelly. "Are there houses of ill-repute where you're from?"

"What's that?"

"No worries, buddy, no worries," Jesse said. "I'm going to show you the time of your damn life. Gonna be like two sailors out on leave. That's right. That's just what we're going to do."

The cashier turned her head away from the television as a news report came on.

The reporter talked about a serial killer on the loose. White male, black baseball cap and glasses.

Rosie paid no mind to the broadcast, she walked to the front door and flipped over the closed sign.

The West Oakland sky had darkened, leaving blood orange hues of pollution on the horizon.

"Look at this shit," Jesse said as they walked down the street outside the liquor store. He shook his head as he gazed upon the abandoned storefronts and houses covered in graffiti. "Street art, my ass. Bunch of crap. Broken windows. Broken condoms. Broken lives. The fuck is wrong with these people?"

Kelly looked unnerved as the light in front of them turned red.

"Come on," Jesse said, crossing against the light. "What are you a Boy Scout?"

Kelly squinted as he looked up at the red light.

"Let's go, dude."

The light turned green and he continued to follow Jesse, not knowing why.

"Where you parked?" Jesse asked.

"I don't have a car."

"You walked? This is a dangerous place for a white boy. I mean we can walk down the streets here in Oakland and nothing will happen to us. Maybe. But absence of evidence isn't evidence of absence. We walk around here long enough someone will try and rob us. That's why we have to stick together. Can't be walking around alone, just one white boy against ten of them-"

"I take the bus," Kelly said. "I have a disability."

"Disability? What kind?"

"Mental."

"Like, you see psychiatrists and shit?"

"Yes, sir."

"Are you crazy?"

"No, sir. I just see and dream about things. And I do things. Sometimes I can't remember if it was real or a dream."

"But you do see a psychiatrist?"

"Yes, sir."

"They worth the money?"

"County pays for it. Plus I get a free bus pass."

"Right on," Jesse said. "Hey, if everyone else in this city gets freebies so can we. People around here are so ugly they make my eyes hurt. They can give them all the welfare they want as long as I don't have to see them. Man, if I were president I would change things, that's for shit-sure. I would test out bio-weapons here. You know, chemicals and shit. Release it into the atmosphere, turn these assholes into mutants. Kinda like the Island of Dr. Moreau. It would be awesome."

"Yes, sir."

"Well, will you look at that."

The two stop in front of a parked Mercedes. Jesse pointed at the bumper sticker that read "Co-Exist" and "Peace."

"See that's what I'm talking about," Jesse said. "Can you believe this shit? Perfectly good German car and they put all that shit on there. Co-exist? Muslims are taking over our damn country and we got assholes with bumper stickers promoting-"

Working himself into a fury, Jesse kicked in the rear brake light before finishing his sentence.

The car alarm went off and startled Kelly.

"Teee haaaawww!" Jesse said, smashing in the other brake light. "Come on!"

Kelly followed Jesse as they ran over to a dilapidated Toyota Camry across the street. The license plate read BAD AZZ.

"This is me," Jesse said, walking to the passenger side door and unlocking it. "Saw the license plate and just had to have it."

"I can't go with you, sir."

"Why not? I think you're cool."

"I don't know you, sir."

"I ain't a fag. Do you think I'm a fag?"

"No, sir."

"Well, let's do this," Jesse reached into his back holster and took out his gun, taking the clip out and then shoving it back in. "Now get in the fuckin' car and let's get rowdy like good sailors should."

Kelly nodded and got into the vehicle.

"Nice to see you changed your mind," Jesse said, hiding the gun in his back pocket again. "Only fools and the dead never changed their mind."

CHAPTER THREE

Jesse drove down the street like a maniac, alternately speeding up then slowing down. He swerved in front of cars, flipping the bird indiscriminately.

Kelly stared straight ahead looking scared shitless.

"Look man, I didn't mean to pull the gun on you," Jesse said. "I promised you a good time, right? We gonna get some whores. Show you what a cool guy I am. How's that sound?"

Kelly shrugged his shoulders.

"The Warriors ain't playing tonight," Jesse pointed at Kelly's baseball cap. "You watch the game last night?"

"No."

"Me neither," Jesse said. "Shit, why do that when you can go out and get some poontang, you know what I mean?"

Jesse looked out the side window and saw a redhead woman walking down the street. Dressed in business attire, her suit did little to conceal her figure.

"Holy shit!" Jesse slowed the vehicle down. "Curves for days!"

The woman turned her head and looked at the men staring at her.

"Hey darlin'" Jesse said.

Rolling her eyes, the woman turned around and began walking in the opposite direction.

"Well, fuck you then," Jesse laughed. "We could have you cumming instead of going, ain't that right, friend?"

Looking up ahead, Jesse saw a brunette walking, her eyes focused on her cell phone.

"Hot, hot, hot," Jesse said. "All these young Cal students out here sometimes. Usually trying to score some dope. What is your type? Me? I don't really have a type. I like them all really. Tall, short. Big ass. Little ass. I just like pulling girls hair. That's what gets me off. It's primal, you know. Doggy style."

They slow down and see a prostitute up ahead. She's redhead, very tall and leaning up against the pole of a bus stop.

Upon seeing Jesse's car slowing down, she twirled around the pole, like a stripper.

"Here we go," Jesse lowered his voice. "Think we might have a live one here."

Jesse stopped the vehicle next to the woman who poked her head in on the passenger side.

"Hey boys, you need a date?"

Her face had pock-marks, as if she had small-pox. Her half-lidded jaundice eyes a dead giveaway of her crack whore status.

Jesse slammed on the gas. "Good God! Did you see that? I've seen ugly but goddamn! And she had no teeth! Then again she doesn't need teeth for what she does!"

Jesse looked over at Kelly and noticed him staring at a different brunette up ahead. The girl stood with her arms crossed, emphasizing her ample cleavage.

"There you go," Jesse said. "There you go."

He stopped the car in front of the woman.

Upon closer inspection, her hair was dark redhead with brown streaks. A light skinned Latina, with full lips and green eyes. In her mid-twenties, she smiled wide as Jesse drove up.

"Two good looking guys in here. How's it going?"

"Will you do the things she won't?" Jesse asked.

"I'm the girl your mami and your papi warned you about," she said. Her voice breathy, with an accented lilt, like a breeze combing through dry leaves on a hot summer night.

"What's good on the menu?"

"That depends on how hungry you boys are," the woman said, reaching down and grabbing Kelly's crotch on 'hungry.'

Kelly shuddered in fear.

"My friend over here is starving," Jesse laughed. "As in he has not had a meal in years, if you catch my drift."

"Well, there will be plenty on the plate for both of you."

"Hop in, *mamacita*," Jesse said.

Kelly watched as the woman got into the car. His heart began to pound and his throat began to feel parched, her sweet perfume quickly filling the vehicle.

Reminding him of his mother.

CHAPTER FOUR

"My name is Maricela," she said from the backseat, looking over at Kelly on the passenger side.

Kelly said nothing, holding the wine bottle to his chest and pursing his lips.

"Is he mute?" Maricela asked Jesse. "Or deaf?"

"He doesn't open up until he really trusts someone," Jesse said. "He's smart that way. Do you always judge people?"

"I'm not judging," Maricela said. "Just asked him a damn question."

"Now you're trying to make him feel bad," Jesse said. "You're supposed to make us feel good. Make me and him feel like kings. Right, Kelly?"

Jesse reached over and playfully hit Kelly in the arm.

"I'll do that and more," Maricela said.

"Damn skippy," Jesse said. "Tee haaawww!"

"You're not high are you?" she asked.

"I'm high on life," Jesse said. "Hangin' with my homie here and about to bust a nut on a fine ass Latina."

"Well, thank you, handsome."

"Here," Jesse reached over and took the wine bottle out of Kelly's hand. "Let's get this party started."

Kelly grabbed the wine back, agitated.

"I didn't mean what I said," Maricela said to Kelly, running her fingers through the hair underneath his cap. "You seem nice. And cute. Sometimes you just know, you know what I mean? You look at someone and you get a feeling about them. It is a survival trait among us escorts."

Kelly pulled back then gave in to the woman's touch.

"There you go," Jesse said. "My friend here is an introvert. Just takes some time before he opens up to you."

"I've seen it all, dude, believe me," Maricela said. "There was this guy the other night who wanted me to shave off his chest hair. And there was this other dude that wanted me to take out this dildo he had shoved up his ass. When I took it out, the dildo was still vibrating."

"Sick fucker," Jesse said. "What a sick fuck."

"Can you imagine shoving a dildo up your ass and than calling an escort to fish it out?" Maricela asked.

"My imagination can't go that far," Jesse said.

"Maybe he called one escort to put it in and then called another to take it out?" Kelly asked.

"There you go," Jesse said. "See? He needs to get to know you before he talks."

"There's my place," Kelly said, pointing in the distance.

The television was already on when the trio stepped inside. A news reporter held up a bottle of Charles Shaw wine, explaining how forensics determined the amount of poison that a serial killer used to murder his victims.

"Nice!" Jesse said as he entered Kelly's house. Faded flowered prints marked the wallpaper but Kelly had no pictures or paintings, only one mirror in the center of the living room.

Maricela walked over to the mirror, dabbing her make-up and adjusting her cleavage.

"This is a nice place, friend," Jesse said. "I can spend lots of time up in here. We can watch TV, play video games, shoot the shit. Do you have an X-Box? My kind of place here."

Kelly said nothing as he entered the kitchen and set the wine bottle down, half-listening as Jesse continued to jabber on.

On the counter, he saw the rat poison and weed killer boxes next to the wine bottle. He quickly grasped the incriminating evidence and shoved them into his trench coat.

"Not a bad view," Jesse said, opening than closing the window curtain. "This place is what blue collar is supposed to look like. Nothing fancy. Just warm coziness. This is America! Shit man, we should go out and get an apple pie to go with that wine."

"You sound like a politician," Maricela said.

"I am the King," Jesse said. "A king. Have you ever been to L.A.?"

"Yeah, I go down south sometimes."

"I was there last month. Hollywood. What a bunch of freaks! I went there thinking I could get away from all these Occupy Idiots and what happens? I get caught up in their protest! Wanted to shoot every one of those tree-hugging bitches!"

Kelly placed the poison inside a cabinet and tried to step back out of the kitchen when Jesse stepped in front of him.

"Freakin' idiots!" Jesse screamed in Kelly's face. "Do you know what I mean? These fuckers should go out and get a damn job. Am I right?"

"Right," Kelly nodded his head.

"That's right, buddy," Jesse said, sidestepping Kelly and entering the kitchen. "What kind of grub you got, man?"

Jesse ignored the ant trail on the counter and opened the refrigerator. "What kind of goodies do we have going on in here?"

Kelly crossed and uncrossed his arms, looking nervous.

"Nice!" Jesse said. "Hey man, there is only one ice cream flavor in the world. Only one. Care to guess?"

Kelly shook his head.

Jesse took out an ice cream carton from the freezer in triumph. "Vanilla! Damn, we have a lot in common."

Jesse opened up one of the drawers and grabbed a spoon.

"Come on," Jesse said. "Let's get the party started."

The two walked back into the living room.

Maricela has her shirt off, standing there wearing nothing but a black bra and jeans.

"Wow," Jesse said.

"You like?"

"Nice artwork," Jesse's eyes scanned up and down Maricela's tattooed body. A snake went down her left arm and she had pentagrams on both shoulders. "You're a devil woman."

"I got into the occult in college," Maricela said, looking down at her own tattoos. "Did a mid-term paper on this occult in Mexico then I got interested in the stuff. This one here is the eye of horus."

Maricela pointed down at her belly-button, the Egyptian symbol of protection inked on her stomach.

"So gentleman," she said. "Are we going one at a time or is this a threesome?"

"My friend here goes first," Jesse said, scooping out a spoonful of the ice cream and letting holding it out to Maricela. "Let's make it special."

Maricela wrapped her lips around the spoon, sucking off the ice cream as she sat down on the chair behind her.

"No," Kelly squealed.

Maricela sprang out of the seat.

"Not that chair!" he yelled.

Maricela stepped away from the chair and gave Jesse a startled look. "Are you sure he's alright?"

"I said don't judge him," Jesse said before taking a few steps back with the young man. "You hearing voices?"

"Loud and clear," Kelly said.

"Alright now," Jesse said. "That's nothing to be ashamed of. You should be proud of that. Been hearing voices all your life and you're still here. You're a damn soldier."

"I am?"

"Hell fucking yeah," Jesse said. "But she'll help you get rid of those voices, okay?"

Jesse patted Kelly on the back before heading into the kitchen.

"Relax, dude," Maricela whispered.

Kelly slowly turned his back to the young woman but she spun him around gently.

"It is really easy," Maricela said, taking Kelly by the hand. "First timers are my specialty."

She lead him to the chair to sit down and he shuddered.

"Easy," Maricela said. "We don't have to do it there."

She placed her hands on both of his shoulders and led him over to the couch.

Kelly sat down, eyes downcast.

Maricela played with unbuckling his belt until he turned away.

"Okay, okay, we can do other things."

She let the strap of her bra fall down off her shoulder.

Kelly looked up with painful shyness, licking his cracked lips as he stared at Maricela's breasts.

"You're a titty man," she laughed. "There you go."

Maricela took his hand and placed it on her left breast, letting the young man knead away.

"Gently," she said, tilting her head back in pleasure. "Gently. There you go. You like that?"

Kelly nodded, noticing the upside down cross that Maricela had tattooed on the underside of her wrist.

"Me too, baby. Me too."

Kelly turned to the kitchen door and shuddered as he saw Jesse standing there, watching.

"What are you doing?" Jesse asked. "I said he is a beginner. He's shy with women. You gotta take it slow."

"You get off on taking a front row seat?" Maricela asked. "We were taking it slow."

"Then why is he so freaked out?"

Maricela glared at Jesse.

"Come on," Jesse said, waving her away from the couch. "Give us a minute here. Go upstairs to the bedroom and we'll be right there. We need to have a man to man."

Maricela got up off the couch, rolling her eyes as she made her way up the steps.

"This always works for me," Jesse said, waving the wine bottle in his hand as he sat down next to Kelly. "Loosens you up. Breaks down whatever blockages you got going on in your big head and little head."

Kelly gulped hard.

"We'll be right there!" Jesse called out. "Go ahead and get nekkid! He'll be right up."

CHAPTER FIVE

Maricela entered the bedroom and closed the door. The lamp on the desk illuminated the neatly made bed. There were pictures of dead bugs on the wall which gave her the creeps. She looked closer and realized that they weren't pictures at all. They were dead moths and butterflies inserted between the glass and cardboard backing.

A buck is a buck, she thought, seeing more than her share of strange. She walked over to the TV set and pushed the button to turn it on, looking for the remote control on the counter.

"Look man," Jesse said, putting his arm around Kelly like a big brother. "There is only one thing you need to know about women, okay? You have to satisfy their needs. Once you do that, you are in. Okay? So do you know what women want more than anything?"

"Help?"

"No, they want to get high," Jesse said, removing his arm around Kelly, struggling to uncork the wine bottle he held between his legs. "You just have to find out what women want. Some women you meet are going to want fun. Power. Status. Money. That is why whores like

Maricela are so great. There is no drama. You pay your fee and get what you want."

Jesse popped the cork on the bottle and Kelly shuddered. He knew he had placed the poison in that one.

Jesse raised the bottle to his lips but Kelly grabbed it out of his hands.

"No!"

Jesse stared at Kelly for a beat.

"You never got to have any fun did you?" Jesse asked.

"She used to send me to the store," Kelly said. "With a note to get booze."

"Your mom?"

Kelly nodded.

"No worries, man," Jesse said, moving closer to Kelly now. "My folks were the same way. Both of them alcoholics. Dad was a functional one. Went to work every day. Worked his ass off every day. Then one day he shot himself. Just stepped into the house and blew his brains out. Died all alone."

"I never knew my Dad. Never. No pictures. Nothing. Bet he died alone."

"My mom didn't even cry," Jesse said. "Just kept bringing men over. Fucked every one. Didn't care if I was listening or watching or what. Definitely didn't care that my Dad found out. She was evil, man. Evil incarnate."

"Mine too," Kelly whispered, hunching his back as of the ghost of his mother could hear him.

"Mine was worse than an evil step mom. She was a real mom."

Maricela laid on the bed, noodling around on her cell phone which now showed a dead battery. Looking around for an extension so she could recharge it, the screen shot on the television caught her eye.

The report showed a police sketch of a man that resembled Jesse.

"Police said to be on the lookout for the license plate BAD AZZ in a late model white or gray Toyota. If you have any information regarding the suspect please call 911 immediately."

Maricela toggled on her cell phone again. Dead.

She ran over to the bedroom door but when he opened it she saw Jesse standing outside with Kelly behind him.

"Someone is in a hurry to get started," Jesse said. "If you're that horny you can go ahead and start without us."

"Was just wondering where you guys were," she said.

"He's ready and rarin' to go," Jesse said, placing his arm around Kelly and shaking him. "Go get 'em, Tiger."

Maricela forced a smile, stepping aside to let the men in.

"You ready to show him a good time?" Jesse asked.

"But of course," she said, her voice quavered, betraying her nervousness. "Give the man a little privacy."

Maricela took Kelly by the hand and led him further into the bedroom. She attempted to close the door but Jesse stopped her.

"Nothing goes on behind closed doors around here," Jesse said.

Kelly looked back at Jesse as if he were about to go into the electric chair.

"You can do it, buddy!"

"Come on, handsome," Maricela motioned for Kelly to sit down on the bed. The young man took a deep breath, eyes downcast until he slowly looked up at woman stroking his upper thigh. "Do you think I'm pretty?" she asked.

Kelly could only nod his head, smitten by her beauty.

"Thanks," she said.

Jesse made as if he were going down the steps but stopped at the top, kneeling down so he remained out of Maricela's eyeline.

He listened to Maricela's voice, his heart beating in anticipation of what came next just like when his mother had men over at the house.

"You look like a movie star," Kelly blurted out. "Like you should be in porn or something."

"We should go someplace else," Maricela said. "Just the two of us. Okay?"

"But what about my friend? You don't like him?"

"I like you better," she said, kissing him on the lips then hugging him.

Kelly shuddered in delight.

"You have to leave," she said, nuzzling his ear. "This dude is a serial killer. Okay? He'll kill us both."

"What the hell is going on here?" Jesse asked stepping through the door, his entire body an antennae telling him that something was up.

"This young stud is pitching up a tent!" Maricela said, standing back up and pointing at Kelly's crotch.

Jesse grabbed her wrist before she could walk back downstairs. "Where are you going?"

"I have to get us some protection. Duh." Maricela hurried out of the bedroom.

Jesse sat down next to Kelly. "What did she say to you?"

"She has a crush on me."

"Ha!" Jesse laughed. "See? See what happens when you give women what they want. You gonna start listening to me now?"

They both hear Maricela's high heels running down the steps.

Jesse sprinted down the stairs and caught her just as she reached the door.

He spun her around, angry. "It ain't polite to leave a party early! Thought you were going to get some protection?"

"I left the rubbers in the car."

"Left the rubbers in the car, bullshit!" Jesse slammed her against the wall. "You're a damn devil. A thief!"

Jesse reached inside Maricela's purse and pulled out a wallet.

Kelly's wallet.

"Stop!" Kelly said, coming down the steps.

"Lifted it straight outta your pocket, dude!" Jesse threw the wallet back at Kelly.

Maricella ran over to the wine bottle on the coffee table and smashed it against the edge. Grasping the bottle by the handle, she held it in front of her as a weapon.

"Ooooh," Jesse said. "Come on, bitch! Come on, let's see what you got!"

Maricela's face contorted into that of feral woman, fighting for her life. She stabbed at Jesse, lacerating his hand with the glass.

"Bitch!" he said.

Maricela ran toward the kitchen.

Jesse gave chase until Kelly jumped on his back.

"Leave her alone!" Kelly screamed.

Jesse threw off the little man with ease, pushing him into the chair. "You crazy? This bitch just tried to rob you, man!"

Racing through the kitchen, Maricela opened the cellar door and locked it behind herself.

"Bitch!" Jesse screamed, pounding on the wood. "Bitch!"

He kicked the cellar door again and again.

"Fuck off!" Maricela cried out.

Jesse looked down at his hand, his blood dripping on the kitchen floor.

Walking back into the living room, he saw Kelly sitting on the couch watching TV, another wine bottle in his hand.

"Dude!" Jesse said, holding up his bloodied hand. "Look what your damn girlfriend did to me."

"She's not my girlfriend."

"Where's the key to your basement?" Jesse asked, taking out his gun. "Or do I have to just blow shit open?"

"I have the key," Kelly said, glaring at Jesse.

"Hey man," Jesse said. "You're looking at me with some hate in your eye. I told you that girl was a thief. A demon. You see that upside cross on her wrist? She's a devil worshiper! Doesn't Satanism freak you the fuck out? Let's go kill her ass."

"She's already dead," Kelly said, staring off into the distance, in his own world.

"All of mine are dead too," Jesse said pointing the gun at his own temple. "So let's kill another one."

"She told me she loved me."

"Of course," Jesse said. "I knew that. That's why I got her for you. Figured she was just your type."

He took the wine bottle out of Kelly's hand and guzzled it down. "Aaaaahhh!"

Kelly returned his attention to the television, his eyes transfixed.

"What is it, goddamnit?" Jesse asked, turning toward the TV. He saw the police sketch of himself and the license plate.

BAD AZZ.

Enraged, he shot a bullet through the TV.

CHAPTER SIX

Maricela heard the gunshot. Startled, she looked around the cellar for a weapon of any kind. She found a fire poker in the corner and gripped it hard.

Kelly ran back toward the cellar door with the keys in hand. "I'll get you out," he called out to Maricela. "I'll help you."

Jesse chased after him but fell down, the room spinning, his entire body sweating. He retched again, with blood streaked bile coming out of his mouth. He looked at Kelly staring at him, wild-eyed with fear. His friend went in and out of focus, doubling and distorting like a kaleidoscope.

What was in that wine?

Maricela took the fire poker and smashed out the tiny cellar windows.

"Help me!" she screamed. "I've been kidnapped! Help me!"

Kelly put the key in the cellar lock but could not get it to open.

Jesse pitched forward over the sink and retched again.

"The fuck you put into that wine?" Jesse asked, purple bile spilling out of his mouth.

"I'm sorry," Kelly said.

Falling to the ground, Jesse pointed the gun at Kelly.

"I was just trying to be a good friend," Jesse said.

Maricela screamed as she heard the gunshot.

She scrambled back up the cellar steps. Pressing her ear to the door, she waited several minutes before she unlocked it.

Opening up the door, she saw both Jesse and Kelly on the floor in a growing pool of blood.

Kelly laid on his stomach, the blood spewing forth from the fatal gunshot blast into his belly. He stared straight ahead at Jesse who laid on his back, blood and foam caked around his lips, neck and chest.

Ants began to scuttle over their bodies.

They were both locked in a death stare at each other. The pupils of their eyes like black holes eating the whites.

Their once lonely faces no longer dark but relieved.

They didn't have to die alone.

STRAITJACKET

TERRY KING

PROLOGUE

They stood in the second story loft of the church. A place where Father O'Malley would go to pray and ponder the problems of the world. He would look through the stained glass windows at the parking lot below and the trees in the park. He think and dream that somehow, someway the words he spoke to his congregation mattered.

The bullets dropped to the ground, echoing throughout the room.

Sister Mary sighed hard as she picked up the bullets and handed them back to the priest.

O'Malley began inserting the projectiles into the chamber of the gun. His hands shaking, he dropped one of the bullets to the ground again.

The nun took the gun out of his hand and picked up the bullet. Shaking her head in disgust, she began loading the chamber, holding out her hand for him to give her the rest of the bullets.

"You know this is all ironic," he said. "My father killed himself. So did my grandfather. Mom's side though."

Sister Mary narrowed her eyes and angled her head to get better eye contact with the priest. She gave him a tight-lipped smile.

"Like father, like son."

"You know this is a sin," he said. "To murder yourself. But I like to think the world murdered me. I tried. I heard every confession. I visited every family. But no one. No one ever thought of me. The person on the inside, do you know what I mean?"

"Of course."

"I never married obviously," the priest said. "I married others. I counseled others. My parents are dead. My brother is on the east coast. He's in a rest home. Just where they want to put me now. They want me to spend the rest of my days staring at that door. Waiting for someone from my past to come visit. Someone who will come in and say 'you were a good man.' But that person will never come. And I'll slowly lose my mind. Just like my brother. I cannot deal with that. I don't want to. It isn't fair."

"You don't have to explain."

"They say it is the ultimate selfish act. But sometimes it is okay to be selfish. Especially when you never thought of yourself. It just kills you inside. The loneliness. The-"

O'Malley took off his priest collar in mid-sentence and tossed in on the chair in front of him. Then he took of his glasses and laid them aside his Bible.

"I read the damn thing cover to cover," he said. "Never really spoke back to me."

"It is the silence," the nun said. "The silence that comes after the trauma that kills you. That is what pours salt in the wound."

"No," the priest said. "I like silence."

She handed the gun back to the priest, her elbows locked as he took the weapon. Her shoulders were hunched; her lips squeezed tight. She peered at the priest as if through a pair of gun slits.

He stared at the weapon for a long, long time. He looked up again at Sister Mary.

The red-headed nun's whole face relaxed; her eyes widened and her forehead unfurrowed. Her cheekbones lowered, her freckles glowing in the low light.

The priest thought her facial expressions were a beautiful thing to watch. Her eyes were like a cloud passing from a mountain lake of deepest blue.

"Don't be afraid," she said.

Then, without warning, he brought the gun to his mouth and pulled the trigger.

CHAPTER ONE

Todd sat slouching in the car, waiting behind the wheel of his car for the longest red light in Detroit. His seventeen year old green Saturn rattled in place, fighting against the Michigan cold. He looked in the rear view mirror at his reflection. He was a square-shouldered, broad shouldered, lantern-jawed man. He had let his military buzz cut grow out a full quarter of an inch but saw the bald spot at the crown of his head. At the age of forty-eight, he looked ten or twenty years older depending on the time of day.

He passed the time by sifting through the crime scene photos on his Ipad. He stared at the picture of the priest laying on the ground with the gun between his fingers.

That looked odd, he thought. Usually when someone killed themselves the gun would be a few feet away from the impact. The next photo showed a full shot of the room. The priest laying on the ground. Plastic sheets covered the windows behind him. Soot covered the far wall with a wooden chair in the middle.

A picture of loneliness.

Todd Richards knew something about that. He felt less like a man who deserved more out of life than a peasant on a sled whipping his dogs forward in the cold.

He clicked on his screen and zoomed in on the priest. The poor old man laying on his right side, blood pooling on the dusty floor beneath him.

The third photo showed the Bible on the chair. His white collar and the glasses beside it.

The next slide showed a picture of the convent. Two large connecting homes with brown stripes going down the sides. The convent sat behind a snow covered road with two leafless trees standing in front of the building.

The light turned green and he tossed the Ipad back onto the passenger seat.

A homeless black man hobbled in front of his vehicle, forcing him to brake. The man wore a light brown jacket with what looked like oil stains all over, like he spent all day sleeping under eighteen wheelers.

The man easily tipped the scales at over three-hundred pounds, unusually well fed for a homeless person.

The man yawned as he made a motion for Todd to roll down his window. Todd recognized the man as "Shamu", a nicknamed he earned from his fellow police officers who noted that the obese homeless man had two front teeth missing. When he opened his mouth, his two remaining teeth gave him the look of the walrus at Sea World.

"Spare some change so I can get something to eat?" Shamu demanded.

"Looks like you've had enough to eat," Todd said, swerving around the fat homeless man and speeding off.

"Fuck you, mother fucker!"

Todd laughed as he watched Shamu gesticulate in his rear view mirror, no doubt cursing up a storm.

He turned on his radio and remembered that the FM band no longer worked. He didn't want to listen to any more talk radio on the AM dial so he flipped the switch to CD mode.

Sifting through the selections, he found a catchy tune. A tune that his teenage daughter used to play all the time when she joined her church's youth group. He remembered how she would sing in their car on the drive over and how he would just laugh. He hated the music but loved his daughter's voice.

> *I'm not ashamed to let you know*
> *I want this light in me to show.*
> *I'm not ashamed*
> *to speak the name of Jesus Christ.*
> *What are we sneaking around for?*
> *Who are we trying to please?*
> *Shrugging off sin,*
> *apologizing like we're spreading*
> *some kind of disease.*
> *I'm saying, "No way. No way."*

Todd found the convent with GPS. He looked up and wondered why no one had taken care of it. Vines were growing up on the wall and all of the windows were shuttered. Supposedly, it was on the city's restoration list and historical sites.

He lit a joint and took a couple of hits, enjoying the stark silence of a cold, snow-filled morning. He looked up at the convent again. Old would be the only word to describe it. Two separate oblongs with faded paint, two stories each, connected in the middle by a small walkway.

Finishing off the blunt, he stepped outside the car and walked straight to the front door.

Todd took out the keys from his pocket and fumbled it into the lock.

Nothing doing. Wrong key.

He then began knocking on the door. Polite at first then harder when he received no answer.

"Mother fucker," he muttered as he began feeling the chill in his bones. He took a few steps back and looked up at the windows on the second story.

"Anybody home?" he called out, laughing to himself.

He ran around the corner of the house and tried the back door. No dice.

Then he went over to the back door of the adjoining house and found the lock to be rusty. He forced it ajar and stepped inside.

He found himself in what he deduced was the former kitchen and pantry. He stepped over dirty white sheets, feeling spider webs hit his face as he ventured further in. He brushed them away then watched a rat scurry under the oven.

Todd walked around to the adjoining foyer and tried the door that connected this part of the convent to the main area of the church. Across the way and through the yellowish tint of the window, he could make out the church pew. There he saw a nun kneeling on one of the benches. She massaged the back of her long neck with one hand, then turned a page of a homily book with the other. Then she bowed her head, clasped her hands, and took on a posture of prayer.

He knocked at the window, trying to get her attention.

She didn't look up or acknowledge him.

"Hello?"

He pounded on the glass again then the wood, creating a racket that sounded like someone violently battering a cookie sheet.

The nun did nothing as she kept her head bowed in prayer.

"Bitch," he said as he walked out of the backroom and back to his vehicle, his feet stomping through a field of dead leaves.

The car didn't start initially. The engine huffed and puffed but didn't kick over. He looked up at the convent, feeling as if the the large windows were evil eyes staring down at him. Finally, the engine started and the car drove off in the snow, slow at first as if it were stuck in second gear, the lure of the convent like a magnet drawing it back.

Todd piloted the Saturn down a long, curvy road, traveling another half mile down to Saint Elizabeth's church. He stepped out of his car and walked through the open doors. Organ music blared as he entered the hall and walked down the aisle.

"Services are over," he heard a voice behind him.

Turning around he saw a priest, tall with curly white hair and black-rimmed glasses. "I'm Father McGuigan. Can I help you?"

"I sure as hell hope so," Todd said. "The archbishop gave me the wrong key to the convent. I need a key that actually opens the door."

"He can't give you the key," the priest said, scratching his head as he lifted his chin like a rooster. His shock of white hair and pale skin complexion made Todd think of powdered donuts.

"Why the hell not?" Todd said, holding up his badge. "It is office police business now. I'm investigating the suicide of one of your priests. Father O'Malley."

"What?"

"Do I have to repeat myself in Latin?"

"No," the priest said, his bushy white eyebrows raised as if he were in shock. "I just didn't think that it was going to be investigated."

"It doesn't smell right," Todd said. "A priest breaks into an abandoned convent and is found with his brains blown out. It looks like a suicide, sure. But we like to be sure and now it looks even more fishy when I can't get into the fucking place. Now are you going to give me the right key or are we waiting for the Pope to bless it first?"

"The Pope can't help you," McGuigan said. "That old convent is abandoned for a reason."

"Yeah, why's that?"

"It is haunted."

"Haunted?" Todd raised his eyebrows and suppressed a laugh.

"Demons."

"Are you fucking serious?" Todd asked. "I am going to say this real slow so that you can understand...I...need...the....key."

"You need to do your research on the place," McGuigan said, his busy, semicircular eyebrows glided up and down, his forehead creased and uncreased as he spoke. "It has always been haunted. It hasn't been occupied in years. Decades. There was a nun. She committed suicide in the same room where you found O'Malley. She pledged her loyalty to the devil and hung herself."

"Your church attracts the winners doesn't it?"

"She sold her soul to the devil."

"I hope she got a good bargain."

"It started after that night,"

"What started?"

"The hauntings," the priest said. "Screaming at night. Voices coming from unoccupied rooms. Messages written in blood on the walls. Excrement smeared everywhere."

"Sounds like a homeless shelter."

"After the nun's suicide they closed down the convent. No one has been inside ever since, except apparently Father O'Malley."

"I need the key, Father." Todd lowered his voice and tried a more polite tact. "Please."

The priest looked Todd over and then reached into his pocket. He took out a silver key out of his chain and handed it to the detective.

"I know you're not a believer," the priest said. "And you think it is all bullshit. But I advise you to please be careful."

"Always," Todd said, moving toward the door. "And don't worry about me. I spend all damn day and night chasing down drug dealers and thugs. Been shot at more times by those human cockroaches than I can remember. It'll be a breath of fresh air to take down an evil spirit for a change. Demons are the real cockroaches. They never die."

Todd flipped the key in the air and caught it.

CHAPTER TWO

Todd drove back through the neighborhood, idling at the light a block before the convent. He clicked on the CD and listened to his daughter Gwen's favorite song again, the memory of his fall from grace gathering gloomily on the Detroit horizon like the growing snowstorm.

He drove another block and reached the convent.

He marched straight up to the door, preparing to raise holy hell if the key didn't work this go around.

Perfect fit. He twisted and turned the knob.

The door creaked open and he stepped in, greeted by another cobweb sticking to his forehead. He wiped the webbing away and felt a chill go up his spine as he looked around the place.

The words of the priest echoed through his head but he didn't want to admit it. He felt a vibe in the place, a sense of coldness and misery. The paint on the walls were long past faded. A broken chair stood near the side wall. A few paintings dotted the furthest wall with an inch of dust on the canvas.

He heard the creaking of footsteps to the side and he spun around fast.

Looking at the stairwell, he watched as the young nun walked down. The same nun as before, her eyes staring at him, unblinking.

"Don't be afraid," she said.

"I saw you before," he said, pointing at the window across the way. "You didn't hear me banging on the glass over there."

She didn't answer immediately as Todd's facial expression betrayed his attraction to her. She had long red hair with crystal blue eyes. He noticed that the nun had a far-away look, like someone blinded from birth. He likened her face to that of an angel, perfectly symmetric with no make-up to soil her innocence.

"I was praying," she said, her hands clasped palm to palm just below her breasts. She looked more like a a college cheerleader than a nun, ready to deliver a cheer or dance a pirouette. Instead, she aimed her half-lidded gaze down at Todd.

"I knocked at the window and you ignored me. What the hell are you doing here?"

"I was a novice here," she said. "I came back to see how things were. This place has a lot of memories for me. I'm Sister Mary."

"You're very pretty," he said, the words coming out involuntarily.

"Thank you," she said. Her face blushed a deep red which made her freckles glow even in the low light.

Smitten by her beauty, he couldn't help but feel at ease by the sound of her voice. Comforting and sweet, she could speak softly and her words would still carry. Lightning flashed outside the window and his mind was pierced by an image of him and the nun on the floor in athletic carnal congress.

He shook his head to snap out of it.

"Are you okay?" she asked.

"I'm Todd Richards," he said, adjusting his voice to a more pleasant tone rather than the standard dickhead detective. "You have the keys to get in here?"

"I have a spare," she said. "But old places like these have many secret doors. Places that are unexplored and no one knows how far they go."

"Haunted houses don't have secrets. Only people. I'm assuming you know about the history of this place?"

"The history?"

"It is supposed to be haunted."

"It was a convent," she said. "Not a haunted house."

"I spoke to a Father McGuigan over at Saint Elizabeth's. He told me the whole story."

"I don't know him."

"Do you know who I am?"

"A man who believes in haunted houses."

"Not me," Todd laughed. "The priest. Says this place is possessed. Evil spirits, demons. Warned me if I didn't watch out some ghost is gonna come flying up my ass."

"Ghosts," she said. "We all have our own ghosts. We leave things behind in a figurative sense. Would you agree?"

"I'm just here to find answers."

"Of course. The cop following the protocol."

"How'd you know I was a cop?"

"I saw the bulge," she approached him. "Of your gun."

He looked straight into her eyes, wanting to avert his gaze but being unable to.

"You really think I'm pretty?"

Todd nodded his head.

The nun gave him a tight-lipped smile and turned around. "I must be going. Watch out for those ghosts, Mister Policeman."

She gave him one last, long appraising look then went back up the stairs.

Todd waited until she reached the top. Then he followed her up.

The large stained glass window at the top of the stairwell let in the only light in the place. Todd reached the top of the steps and tried a light switch in the corner to no avail. He turned left and headed down the dark hall. He passed three closed doors, creaking one open to see the empty room of a nun's old quarters.

He closed the door and continued on. At the end of the hall he saw a statue of Mother Mary with blood-stained tears running down her face.

To his right, he noticed that the last door at the end of the hall stood slightly ajar.

Had she gone inside there?

Pushing the door open, he recognized the room as the one in which the priest had been killed. The furniture looked the same, with the chair in the middle of the room. He looked on the floor and saw the chalk outline of the priest's body. Todd remembered how the man laid sideways in a fetal position as if he were a grieving baby.

Todd buttoned his jacket as he began to feel a chill. The entire room felt as if it were dropping

ten degrees and he could now see his own breath.

Then came the smell.

He had to hold his breath as the stench of excrement filled the air. He looked at his shoes, at first thinking that he stepped into something.

Voices could be heard in the distance, sounding like they were coming from the next room.

"Hello?" he called out. "Anybody here?"

The light from the chandelier above began to flash.

Todd looked up and saw the light fixture crash down as he moved away just in time.

He froze in place, looking up at the hole in the ceiling. The house remained completely still. He could only hear the sound of his own breathing and the creaking of his own footsteps as he ran down the steps and out the door.

CHAPTER THREE

"Okay," Todd said as Father McGuigan led him back into his study. "Tell me more."

Todd didn't admit to what happened. He felt spooked, no doubt about it. He didn't see another trace of the nun that greeted him at the steps. The chandelier nearly decapitating him didn't stick in his mind as much as the complete silence of the convent, like a living tomb waiting to swallow him up.

"You look like you saw a ghost," the priest said, sitting down at his desk. His study consisted of a small table and a laptop computer. Two empty wine coolers were at the center of the table and the priest followed Todd's eye.

"They're less fattening than beer," the priest patted his ample pot belly.

Various books stood in piles on the far wall and Todd couldn't help but notice that the majority of them had the word "exorcism" in the titles.

"What more can you tell me about Father O'Malley? Why did he go back to an abandoned convent to kill himself?"

"O'Malley was a decent man," McGuigan said. "Cared very much for people. Funny thing is that when he was younger he actually looked like Jesus. The redhead, blue eyed version. But he always seemed uptight, as if his skin was stretched too tight over his skull. He was always smiling but his eyes were watery, which I always attributed to his sad childhood. His father committed suicide before him. So I think along the way he developed a crisis of faith. A dwindling church going population and indifference did him in. But he was strong and I figured he accepted those things as part of the journey. I just didn't see a suicide coming at all. Goes to show you how you never really know someone."

"But again," Todd said, trying hard to remain patient. "What was he doing there? Did he go there a lot?"

"I don't see what business he had there," McGuigan said. "But I haven't talked to him in ages. We had a few e-mail correspondence and a phone call or two over the past year. He didn't say much. Just said to pray for him. He was battling some personal demons."

"Well, the personal demons beat him. What did he say in his e-mails?"

"Not a whole lot. Just enough to let me know that things were bothering him. I know he suffered a minor stroke. He rehabbed and began to walk again. Didn't affect his speech too much when I talked to him. He was the head priest over at our sister church, Saint Phillip's. The church attendance was dwindling though. He had little to no attendance by the time he rehabbed back."

"So that's it? He offed himself because no one wanted to listen to him anymore?"

"You can't judge him," McGuigan said. "He had a tough life. Put up with a lot. He got old and thought no one cared. I should have reached out more."

"And he sent you an e-mail before he killed himself?"

The priest nodded. "I don't know why he went there. He just said I would find his body there and that his life savings was mine. Didn't want it to go to the church, for whatever reason. Five grand in case you're wondering."

"Did he know the convent was haunted?"

"Everyone does. The Catholic church recorded all of the exorcisms that took place there. The place has been declared as possessed. Evil."

"Why not tear it down?"

The priest shrugged his shoulders. "Everyone is afraid of the damn place."

"No one outside the church really believes the story though, right?"

"The thing is, when you say haunted house you think ghosts and goblins and things that go boo in the night. But there are certain places that you go, certain places that trigger memories inside you that are better left in the past. That's what makes the place haunted."

"Well, I met someone there who can't stay away from the place."

"Who?"

"A nun."

"A nun?"

"Said she used to live there. I saw her praying in the altar."

"Are you serious?" the priest gave him a solemn look as if seeing him for the first time.

"That's my line."

"Did she give you her name?"

"Sister Mary. Mid-twenties. Cute. I mean real cute. Had these milky blue eyes. I thought she was blind at first."

"Sister Mary-" Father McGuigan looked lost in thought for a beat. "What else did she say?"

"Just said the place wasn't haunted and that she goes there all the time. Don't see what for, the mess is in shambles."

"There isn't another convent within twenty miles from here."

"Maybe she drove over."

"Did you see another car outside?"

"So you're the detective now?"

"I'm saying that the convent closed in the early 1900s. Impossible for her to serve there. She's lying."

"Well, maybe she was confused. Or schizophrenic. Could have been some college student with a fetish for dressing up as a nun."

"You have to stay away from that place," the priest said, standing up. "The devil. He is a great deceiver. He comes as an angel of light. That is what you saw back there."

"Holy fuck," Todd shook his head. "No, that nun wasn't the devil."

The priest shook his head in futility. "Okay, fine. You're right. Probably a college student playing a prank."

"You have been watching way too many movies, Father. 'The Exorcist' was just a movie-"

"You were there," McGuigan said. "I know you felt it. It's real. That uneasy feeling you got when you entered the place. That sixth sense going off in your hind brain telling you that this place is nowhere you should be? That feeling you got that someone was watching you?"

"A demon was watching me?"

"The devil is real. You saw or felt something there and now you come to me for answers. Well, I'm giving you one. What you saw was the Prince of Lies."

"She was a nun," Todd said. "Had the penguin outfit and everything."

"You mock," McGuigan said. "Trust me, the devil is not mocked."

"There are no demons," Todd said, walking down the hall. "The only demons we create are in our own mind. And if we're not careful, we end up committing suicide in an empty convent."

The priest followed him out the door and extended his hand.

Todd noticed the loose grip of the priest. His hand cool and dry, all papery skin and knobbly knuckles. The priests long fingers reached nearly all around Todd's hand.

"Be careful," the priest whispered.

Todd skipped down the church steps think how McGuigan may have been the palest person he had ever seen. He thought of bringing the man under the light so he could see his bones.

A part of him wanted to believe what McGuigan said. He had been raised Catholic and drifted from the faith, thinking that the teachings were redundant. But the Gothic symbols of the church always scared the shit out of him and he resented it. Demons, devils, gargoyles and everlasting damnation. It was all meant to scare young kids into being believers for life.

He looked back at the church, a tall building with a golden painted cross on the roof.

Demons still scared him, real or imagined. He wished there were a higher being to protect him against everything dark in the world.

CHAPTER FOUR

Todd sat inside the Denny's restaurant alternating between looking out the window and looking at the wrinkled picture in his hand.

A picture of his wife and daughter. Gina or "Little Jeanie" as he used to call her, must have been twelve years old in the photo. She still had that bright and loving smile. He remembered how she used to look at him in awe and loved spending time with him.

Gwen changed over time. They all do, he thought, trying to comfort himself. They had fought a lot after she turned sixteen but it was typical teenage rebellion stuff.

His wife had the same look in the picture. A happy, tender and caring facial expression. That is how he wanted to remember her.

But he couldn't control how they remembered him.

Especially his daughter. The memories of her waxed and waned like the moon-always there but not always accessible because of the pain he experienced while thinking about her.

He caressed her face in the photo with his forefinger.

Time goes by so fast. If I could change things, I would.

"Are you okay?" the waitress came over and poured him a fresh cup of coffee. She had a long, oval face, sharp cheekbones and strawberry redhead hair that she wore in a ponytail. Her name tag read "Paula". She was long legged and hippy in a way that turned Todd on but he was at least fifteen years older than her.

"Sir, are you okay?"

"No," he said, folding the photo back up as if he wanted to crush it, his eyes flicking angrily back and forth, Todd shoved the picture back into his wallet as if he were trying to stab something. "Can I get another one of these?" he asked, pointing at the beer bottle.

"I think four is enough," she said.

"Who are you, my wife?"

"You're not married."

"How can you tell?"

"I can tell."

"Really now?"

"And I know its tough," she said, removing the empty bottles from the table and holding them as if they were full of poison.

"What?"

"Whatever it is that you were thinking about."

"I'm not thinking about anything."

"Well, think about this," she said, looking behind herself then back at him. "Life can tough. The universe doesn't care if you're on top of the mountain or down in the gutter. You have to create your own good times. And if you have a few extra dollars on you I can guarantee that you'll have a good time."

"I'll think about it," he said, gazing at her body up and down, trying to assess her curves in her waitress uniform..

"You do that," she said, walking away.

Todd pulled out his cell phone and dialed. He looked at the waitress back at the counter and fantasized about what she would be like in bed. Probably wild and dirty and quick to a fault. She probably had a rough life, had too many children with too many men. The wrong men who broke her moral compass.

"Hello?" came the voice on the other end.

"Jessica?" he asked.

A long, deep sigh on the other end. "Todd. Really? What is it now?"

"Remember awhile back you said to call you if I ever needed to talk," he stammered. "Well, now is one of those times."

"You sound drunk."

"I'm not drunk."

"Then what's wrong?" Jessica said. "Todd, I'm married now, remember? I've moved on. We got a divorce."

"That means we can't talk anymore?"

"That means you can't call me out of the blue and expect me to drop everything to talk to you."

"Oh, right," he said. "How silly of me. After all we been through. I can't even call you anymore. The new guy won't let you talk to the old one so you have to listen to him. Why? Because the new guy has a nicer house. A flashier car. Makes more money and that makes you bought and paid for."

He heard a click on the other end.

Todd got up and picked up his last remaining beer bottle. He fished out a twenty dollar bill from his wallet and tossed the money on the table.

He walked toward the exit, avoiding eye contact with the waitress.

"You okay?" she called out from behind the cashier's desk with a pouty look on her face.

"Never better," he said. "Just got a job to do that's all."

"What do you do?

"I hunt ghosts," he said, stepping out into the cold air. "I'll call you when I get a raise in pay."

CHAPTER FIVE

The beer in Todd's system made him brave.

He took another big swig as he opened the door to the abandoned convent and entered inside. The smell hit him immediately. The old fixtures that remained, the couch, the grotty carpet, the broken toilet, all smelled of stale piss.

Turning on his flashlight, he walked up the steps and reached the room where Father O'Malley had killed himself.

Kicking down the door, he marched in.

A bolt of lightning flashed across the window outside. He felt a sudden chill, colder than before as if he just stepped into a meat locker.

The thunder rumbled above and the sound jolted his memory of his past. That night he drove home through a storm, way past drunk.

That night he came home and opened the door to his wife crying.

"She's dead," he remembered his wife saying.

His heart stopped at that moment.

"Our baby is dead."

His daughter Gwen had been killed by drunk driver that night. Both she and her friend were crossing the street when someone caromed into them and didn't stop, his wife explained.

Both women flipped over the vehicle and cracked their heads on the cold road.

The driver didn't stop.

Because the driver had been Todd.

And he couldn't tell his wife. Or anyone. Ever.

He remembered driving and the rain coming down hard. The lightning flashed across the sky and distracted him. Then he remembered slamming into the two pedestrians. He didn't know if they were men or women.

He just knew he had to run. Another DUI and he would go to jail. And if they were hurt, forget about it. He wasn't drunk enough to realize that his life would be over if he got caught.

So he pressed down on the gas, sped a half-mile away then made a sharp turn.

No witnesses. No crime.

He waited it out for a hour then drove back home, partly sober.

And heard the news.

Todd knelt down beside the chalk drawing on the ground. He rolled onto his side and laid down inside, contorting his body to fit the outline.

"I know how you felt, old man," he whispered. "I know how you felt."

Then he heard the footsteps coming down the hall.

He stood back up, took another swig from his beer bottle and took the holster off his gun.

"Todd?" a woman's voice asked.

It couldn't be.

"Jessica?"

He put his flashlight on her, seeing his wife dressed in a raincoat, standing in front of the door. Soaking wet, the moonlight sparkled over the droplets of water on her face.

"Really chilly in here, Todd."

"What are you doing here?"

"I was in the neighborhood so I thought I'd drop by."

"Its been a long time."

"Too long," she said. "I am sorry I never got back in touch."

"I called you and called you," he said. "I tried. I reached out. I didn't know what to do. When you left me, I was just-"

"I hurt you, I know."

"It didn't have to be that way."

"Nothing ever has to be that way," she said. "But it just is. Most couples don't survive the death of a child. Statistics show that."

She was analytical like that, he thought. A lawyer constantly arguing her case.

"But we could have been different. If we could have just talked."

"I needed to get away," she said. "And then things just snowballed and I met Michael and now I know better. It was my fault. I'm so sorry, Todd."

"It is okay."

"Don't do that," she said. "You always do that. Put your own needs down. I've missed you and I love you. Can you say the same? Can you say that you need me?"

"I never stopped loving you," Todd said.

She walked straight at him, quickly crossing the room. He almost thought she would walk through him until she put her arms around him and held tight.

"Six seconds," she said. "Remember our six second hugs? Because that's how long it takes for the brain chemicals to release the oxytocin. We stopped hugging each other after. That was a big mistake. My mistake."

Todd said nothing. He closed his eyes and enjoyed the warmth of her embrace. He forgot what it felt like to feel her breasts against his chest, the fruity smell of her freshly shampooed hair as it brushed against his cheek.

"I know it was tough for you, too," she said. "I shouldn't have been so hard on you. Should have stuck it out."

"You have a life now," he said. "A different life. I understand. You had to move on. I should do the same."

"But you can't," she said. "And neither can I."

He slowly pushed her back, looking her in the eye.

"What are you saying?"

"I'm saying that I made a mistake. About us. I thought I wanted all of those nice things. Big house. Big car. It just left me unhappy. Because I didn't have you. Or Gwen. I felt empty inside. I couldn't get us out of my mind. Our family. The way things were."

"I know what you mean by feeling empty."

"You filled your emptiness with alcohol. I filled it with stuff. We both handled it in different ways."

"I thought you hated me."

"I never hated you," she said. "I hated what happened. I had to hate something. Blame somebody. I projected all that on to you."

"How did you find me?"

"You told me on the phone."

"No, I didn't."

"Yes, you did!"

"No," he said. "You hung up on me-"

"Stop!" she said. "Let's not fight. Aren't you tired? Tired of fighting."

"That's all we did."

"We needed to do more of this," she said, gently touching her lips against his before letting the touch ascend into a full-blown kiss.

Lightning flashed outside the window again.

Is this really happening? He thought.

She pulled back and nodded her head as if she read his mind.

His wife looked as she did on his wedding night. Innocent, pure and dewy-eyed as they were about to make love for the first time.

"Why wasn't I good enough for you?" she asked.

"You were-"

"But you liked this better," she said, taking the beer bottle from his hand.

The thunder rumbled above.

Todd's skin tightened all over his body. The chill raced up his spine and spread to his extremities, as his entire body felt stiff.

The priest sifted through the old newspaper clippings in the church study.

It has to be here.

Finally, by pure chance, he came upon the article.

"Nun commits suicide," the headline read. The date on the newspaper was December 7, 1912. The priest read the entire account of how the young nun hung herself after going on a bizarre rant about Satan and demon possession. The newspaper showed an old black and white photo of the nun. She had long hair and had a beautiful face, just as Todd had described.

The priest got up out of his chair and paced a few steps thinking. He twirled the backrest of his chair with the tips of his long fingers, setting the chair spinning in place.

Looking over at his phone, he saw the message machine light flashing. He scooted his chair over and depressed the button.

"Father McGuigan," Todd said, his voice slurring. "You were right. I just want you to know that. I know exactly how the priest felt. And you were right. I can't judge him. Hell, I'll probably end up just like him. But I'm calling to confess. Confess my sin. Two years ago, I was drunk. And it was raining and I was driving too damn fast and I struck two kids. Teenagers. One of them was my daughter. I kept driving. I just remember them hitting them so hard they both rolled over the top of my hood. I didn't give aid or stop. I just kept going. Even after I found out it was my own daughter. I had to keep going. It didn't seem real. Just didn't seem real. I drove and drove and when I see teenage girls on the street I see my Gina inside them. Sometimes I think it is her. But I'm calling you now to let you know. If you want to contact the authorities, you can. But I would rather tell you than them. Forgive me, Father. Say a prayer for me. Say a prayer for my daughter. I have to cross a burned bridge now. And I think I know the place to do it."

The priest depressed the button as the message ended.

Without a moment's hesitation, he put on his coat and headed out the door.

The thunder rumbled then the lightning flashed, illuminating the entire room before everything went dark again.

"My neck hurts," his wife said, turning her back to him.

Todd reached out and began massaging her trapezius muscles. Jessica's skin felt cold, mottled and clammy not as warm as before.

"I'm so sorry," she said.

"There's something I have to tell you," he said.

Lightning struck outside the home and thunder rolled in.

She turned back around. To his shock, his daughter now stood before him.

"Gwen?"

"Daddy?" she mocked, her body covered in snow and blood, the red liquid pouring down her forehead.

"What-"

"You killed me, Daddy."

"No!" Todd screamed.

"Yes!"

Todd heard the door slam below then someone running up the stairs.

"No," Todd whispered.

"Yes!" Gwen screamed again, blood poured down her face and into her eyes. "You killed me! You killed me!"

"Todd!" the priest screamed as he entered the room. "Snap out of it! Whatever you're seeing, whatever is in front of you isn't real! He's the Prince of Lies!"

Father McGuigan's face was contorted tight, his eyes so sad that he looked like he could cry at any instant.

The detective spun around and didn't see McGuigan at all. He only saw a reflection of himself in the form of the priest.

He took out his gun and fired once. Then twice. Then he emptied the entire chamber into the priest's fallen body.

EPILOGUE

The coroner placed Father McGuigan into the body bag as the technician snapped one more picture.

"Give me the gun, Todd," the Captain said as he knelt in front of the detective.

Todd stared straight ahead, in another world, with the gun held to his temple.

"Don't be afraid" he mumbled, pulling the trigger again with the empty gun.

Lightning flashed across the window. Thunder rattled the windows of the old convent.

"Don't be afraid. Don't be afraid."

THE SCREAMS OF GHOSTS

ALEXIS RAYE

159

As she was about to close her email for the night and go to sleep, Sara heard that familiar little beep. A new message was waiting for her. It was an email sent through her YouTube account, which she had filtered as soon as her channel had taken off. It was only 9 months ago that she started uploading videos of her adventures but she had really started ghost hunting years earlier. As a kid, she and her brother would dare each other to go into the creepy abandoned houses on the other side of town. They fascinated her with their old architecture and their decrepit walls. She couldn't believe that houses that looked so lifeless, used to be alive with the sounds of families. Somehow, they never scared her, though she pretended to be for her brother.

She truly loved exploring them. What she loved even more was the attention she got from telling her friends about her brave trips inside. She never had enough of that. From the age of 8 and all the way through high school, she regaled anyone who would listen of dark stories filled with supernatural events that she made up off the cuff. Not everyone believed her but it was hard to deny how good of a story teller she was.

And as a new college graduate from a media arts school, she had dedicated her first year of adulthood into creating this persona of an extreme ghost hunter. Her success was overwhelming, even to her, and her fame seemed to grow exponentially every day. She was now even recognized on the street and asked for autographs. That, of course, made all of her sleepless nights and uncomfortable overnight stays in creepy old houses worth it.

The email was still bold as she clicked on it. It was an invitation to fly across the country to Louisiana sent from "The Conservation Collective of Pre-Civil War Phantasmal Plantations". She read it carefully.

Dear Ms. Sara Elliot,

The Conservation Collective of Pre-Civil War Phantasmal Plantations would like to extend an invitation for you and your crew to spend a night in one of our oldest and most spectral houses. It is called "The Lynch Plantation" named after its original owner, although its name holds appropriately with its history. Mr. Lynch was said to be the cruelest man in the south and lynched all of his slaves when he found out that the war had been won by the north. Surprisingly though, his story is not the one that the locals remember. Called Pi Beta Die by the locals, this house's last use was to house a sorority for the local university. 15 years ago, the maintenance man assigned to the house had a psychotic break and killed all 24 members of the sorority then hung himself on the porch outside.

It is our belief that the Lynch Plantation's history is enough to interest you but to further encourage you to create an episode for this house, we have arranged all of your travel and accommodations. You will see the details in the attached document.

The Conservation Collective of Pre-Civil War Phantasmal Plantations seeks to get more publicity and therefore more funding for our cause so please send your reply as soon as possible.

Best Wishes,

The CCPCWPP

She was hooked. Instead of going to bed as planned, she stayed up all night reading and researching the sordid history of the plantation. It was even more incredible, terrifying and mysterious than they had let on in the email. She knew that a night in this house would solidify her as YouTube's leading Ghost Hunter and may even lead to her getting her own show. She knew her fans well. They would love the creepy historical aspect and eat up the sorority massacre with a spoon. When she was too excited to wait, she dialed the number of her main camera tech Lila.

"Its 6:45am Sara, you better have actually seen a ghost," she grumbled. Lila wasn't a morning person and she had known Sara for long enough to know that most of her "ghost sightings" were fake and in fact was one of the people responsible for how real their "encounters" looked.

"Lila, if you wake up now and listen, I'll buy you Starbucks and give you a raise," Sara said. She knew Lila couldn't resist coffee.

"What is it?" she asked, sighing.

Sara beamed with enthusiasm. She knew that it was coming across through the phone because as she explained the email, Lila became more and more alert and excited.

"This could be huge for us Sara!"

"So you're in?" Sara said, knowing that she didn't even need to ask. "Duh!"

"Ok ,we have to get the guys to agree too." Sara coached.

"Just promise them an adventure and to keep them when you get your own show," Lila said nonchalantly. Of course the rest of the crew would agree. The guys were in their mid-twenties and could be pacified with a cheeseburger.

The next few days were filled with preparation. Sara responded to the email to agree to the trip and outlined what she needed when they arrive and explained who she was bringing. The impression she got from the responses were that the more the merrier. Finally, they were all on a plane from Washington to Louisiana. The guys slept the whole way, snoring loudly of course. Sara and Lila sat together to write the script for the background and opening. They would shoot the outside of the plantation and house during the day and have shots of Sara explaining all the details she found about the mass lynching and murders.

By time they arrived, Sara and Lila had all of their shots planned and a script all laid out. Even though they were itching to go straight to the old house, The Conservation Collective of Pre-Civil War Phantasmal Plantations contact insisted they check into a hotel and get settled and rested. They would begin their investigation and shooting tomorrow. They were all smiles and splurged on room service and watched TV on the flat screen. The hotel was obviously very old but well-kept and the rooms were modernized for the guests' comfort. The lobby was small but elegant with two rows of white pillars that led out to the street. After they were stuffed, they decided they needed to walk it off by exploring the bustling town around them.

It was a warm October night so they skipped their jackets and made their way down the old fashioned road. The buildings were tall and thin and the antique street lights cast long shadows against them which no one else seemed to notice. The group weaved their way in and out of the busy streets watching the locals as they enjoyed the many bars and cafes. Andrew, one of the sound techs was mesmerized by the voodoo shops he saw and dragged Colin, another camera guy, in with him. He bought them all incense and they laughed as they all wandered the streets with the potent twigs. Finally they settled on a quiet smoky café. Knowing they had to be awake and alert the next day, they all opted for coffee or tea. As they sipped the delicious, hot beverages, they began to discuss the plan for the next day.

"Ok, I think we should be all packed by 11am. I want to make sure we can get to the location and have plenty of time to explore the plantation before sunset. We also need time to shoot the outside shots with the narrative and set up camp inside for the night," Sara said.

"I agree," Lila said. "Colin, I know you have that 4k camera that can work in low light. Hoorah for that. I was thinking we'll start outside and work our way in. We'll shoot like we always do, start in the living room, I'll explain the history of the house then we'll pretend we'll hear something and head upstairs."

"You want me to add a sound effect in post?" Colin asked.

"Yeah, of course," Lila said. "As long as its not too cheesy. Has to sound real. Like a ghost screaming or something."

"I have no idea what that would sound like," Colin laughed.

Lila covered her mouth and made a groaning sound. "Like that."

"Sounds like a bullfrog with indigestion."

Well, you know what I mean. We'll worry about all that later."

"Done deal."

"Of course, we will have to wait until we see it in person to make the final decisions but Sara and I have pretty much memorized the property maps and house floorplans." Lila finished.

"How creepy is it that it's called "Lynch"?" Andrew said.

Matt, their back-end video editor, chewed on some cookies as Andrew glanced his way.

"What? Just cuz I'm black you look at me?" Matt said jokingly. Andrew gave him a little, playful shove and they laughed.

"I'm just saying..." Andrew said with a laugh, "If there is some sort of evil ghost there... you might be the first to go."

Colin nudged Matt, "Don't worry man, I got your back!" Then they all started laughing.

Sara really enjoyed her crew. They were as silly as they were serious and worked as hard as she did. But they also brought her out of her head and gave her time to be sarcastic and have fun. She smiled at them. Then she saw a young woman lean over to Andrew.

"Excuse me... Uh... were you talking about going to the Lynch Plantation?" she asked, looking more than a little concerned.

Andrew grinned, apparently not picking up on her trepidation. "Yep! First thing tomorrow!"

The blood drained from her face. "Why... why would you go there?" she asked, her voice shaking.

"See that girl over there?" Andrew pointed to Sara. The girl nodded and Sara gave a little wave. "Well she is a ghost hunter and also a tiny dictator. We go where she tells us," he said sarcastically. A tone this young woman missed.

She looked directly at Sara. "You need to stay away from there."

Sara laughed nervously. "Oh come on... It's just a house. We will be there one night and that will be it."

The young woman looked even more terrified. "You're staying the night?!" she asked. Her voice carried enough that the rest of the people in the café turned to look at them. The soft music in the background stopped playing.

Sara and her team suddenly were the center of attention. Something that Sara was only comfortable with when it was filmed, not live. She looked at all the faces staring back at her. "Yea... that was part of the contract. My team and I have been paid to make a show for it... to raise money to restore it. It will bring more tourism to this town."

"Restore it?" the young woman asked. "We don't want it restored and we certainly don't want any tourists coming here only to be killed by going in that house."

The other patrons in the place nodded their heads in agreement.

"Listen, I have been all over the United States. I have stayed in over a hundred haunted houses. Nothing violent has ever happened and no one has ever been hurt." Sara said, choosing her words wisely. She wanted to tell them that all of this ghost business was crazy and that she had never encountered anything supernatural, but she didn't want that to get out and damage her show's credibility.

"All due respect... you've never stayed in this house." Another guy said from the corner. Sara's crew looked around at the petrified faces.

"So none of you ever go there? Even out of curiosity?" Colin asked.

"The last person that went there out of curiosity was found hanging from the porch the next day." The young woman replied.

"Maybe he was depressed and chose to off himself there." Andrew suggested while rolling his eyes. If anyone was a skeptic, it was him.

"He was my brother," she said. Andrew looked mortified and wished his tea had a shot of whiskey in it.

"Oops," he muttered, wishing he could say more.

"I'm sorry for your loss but we were paid to do something and we never back out of a contract." Sara said while Andrew stared at the table in front of him. "Now, I think we should be going." She said as they all stood up.

They shuffled out of the café and began walking towards the hotel quietly. They were all silently trying to brush off the many warnings they had just heard and get their excitement back.

"It's ok guys, some places just really buy into this crap." Lila offered.

"Yeah... but we have never had that reaction from any other location," Matt said. "Those folks are serious about this shit."

"Come on guys," Sara said. "This is a beautiful, creepy, historic building. It's going to be great, AND safe." They were probably just hazing the out of towners. I bet they're probably in there right now laughing their asses off at scaring us. Well, we'll let them think that way."

"Hey, uh... excuse me! Wait!" They heard someone say behind them. They turned. It was another young woman who had been listening silently in the café. She ran up to them and stopped. "Sorry, its just... we were wondering... who paid you to come here?"

"Um, it's a group called The Conservation Collective of Pre-Civil War Phantasmal Plantations. I believe they support and restore these kinds of places all over the south and have a lot in this area. I looked them up, their headquarters is just on the other side of town next to a Piggly Wiggly on 2nd street." Sara replied.

The girl looked around at the group with a strange expression. "That part of town has been completely abandoned for 10 years. There was a hurricane that destroyed it and we didn't have enough money to restore it... and as far as I know, there has never been a group by that name in this area. And I have lived her my whole life. I really don't think you should go to the plantation... someone is setting you up."

Sara looked uneasy but Andrew stepped forward.

"Listen, we appreciate your concern but I am sure there is a reasonable explanation. No one would spend this much money on a prank. Now tell all your buddies at the café that we aren't backing down."

Sara looked at the girl. If anyone had spoken to her like that she would have just let them walk straight into a moving car. But this girl stood there with panic on her face. She knew she couldn't say more but still looked like she wanted to stop them somehow. Her facial expression gave Sara goosebumps but before she could even consider breaking the contract, Andrew and Colin started leading her toward the hotel.

"This town is full of crazies." Matt said under his breath.

CHAPTER TWO

Sara didn't sleep well that night. The scene in the café played in her head over and over. She lay awake listening to everyone else snoring. Finally, she flopped over to look at the clock. It was 3:19 am. She groaned quietly. She thought about how excited she had been for this and managed to talk herself back into the adventure before her, deciding that the townies just didn't get out much and had possibly seen too many movies. She fell asleep.

By 11am exactly, their van was packed and any trace of hesitation from the night before was gone and the silliness had returned. Colin was shooting footage of their drive on his phone. Sara and Lila were taking selfies with all of the equipment. Andrew was driving, as always and Matt was snoozing in the front seat.

After a 40 minute drive, passing through the town, driving past the university, they finally pulled up to a large flat expanse. There was a dirt road jetting off to the left and a large sign above it that was covered in dust. Matt jumped out and managed to jump up to wipe the dust away. Sure enough it said "LYNCH". Colin couldn't help it, and he jumped out to take a picture of Matt standing under the sign with both hands flipping him off and a huge grin. They all giggled and rolled their eyes. Then they took off down the dusty dirt road. The large house grew as they neared it.

"I knew it was a mansion but I guess I didn't think it would be this big." Lila said.

"What do you think a sorority was thinking in buying something like this?" Sara asked.

"Simple, they could have keggers and ragers without the neighbors complaining." Colin said. He was the only one who had been a part of Greek life. A part of his past he tried to suppress.

They pulled up to the front of the house and climbed out. For a moment they just stood, appreciating its old fashion beauty and its size. It was gigantic. The wrap around porch alone was bigger than Sara's apartment. Sara and Matt continued to look over the house and the land while Lila, Colin and Andrew unpacked the equipment. When they finished, Lila walked up to Sara to make a game plan.

"It's hard to believe that the townspeople wouldn't want to save this place. It's so beautiful." Sara whispered.

"I know. Like look over there! Past that field it looks like there is a pond and small wooded area. And this tree over here would be great for a giant swing..." Lila said as she approached an old Oak tree that was closest to the house.

"Its really big. Like really big. This is going to be our best shoot yet," Sara said.

"Where should we start?" Lila asked.

Sara looked around thoughtfully. "Ummm... let's begin with the civil war history of the plantation and slaves with the fields in the background. Then I will walk to the tree and end at the porch when I talk about the sorority massacre. Got it?"

Lila nodded once and set up her camera. She began rolling as Sara started to talk.

"Hello, today we are in Louisiana at their best kept secret haunted destination. The Lynch Plantation is over 200 years old and has a most interesting history. Built by a Slave trader and his wife in the early 1800s, this plantation was one of the largest and most profitable in the area. Although aptly named for the fate of over 300 slaves, the Lynch plantation actually received its name from the slave trader who built it. James and Mary Lynch became exceedingly wealthy from the cotton cultivated here. Once the war was won by the north, they knew that their way of life would never be the same. Already know to be a cruel master, James Lynch decided that his final act of rebellion against the north was to kill all of the slaves he held. Most of them were hung from the branches of this oak tree but the younger children and smaller women were drown in the pond at the back of the property.

Then the bodies were collected, placed in a pile and burned at the entrance where you can still see bits of burn marks today. Only 5 years after the mass lynching, Mary Lynch suffered a psychotic break, claiming that the ghosts of those she helped kill were haunting her. She stabbed her husband and then hung herself on the porch right here. But perhaps the most famous suicide on this porch was that of mass murderer Gary Lindale. Gary, a maintenance man from the university was hired specifically to look after the needs of this house while it served as the Pi Theta Kai sorority house. He lived in a small servant house that used to stand just over there but has since been demolished. One night, Lindale snapped, much like Mary Lynch and went on a murdering spree killing every single sorority girl inside. He then called 911, left the phone off the hook and hung himself in the exact same place as Mary.

This house certainly is one of our more chilling explorations and we invite you to join us for a night at the Lynch Plantation." Sara said and stopped. That was the cue for Lila to stop rolling. It never ceased to amaze her that Sara could do these on the first take with no notes in front of her. She was a natural.

"Let's say we explore, take pictures and maybe some landscape footage?" Sara asked Lila and Colin.

Andrew and Matt were right behind, having a heated debate about which sorority girls they thought were the best partiers. Sara and Lila tuned them out, focusing on the expanse in front of them. The sun beat down and even in mid-October, the heat made them sweat. For a moment, Sara imagined what it would have been like to harvest in this heat as a slave. She let herself mourn the loss of the hundreds of innocent lives. She didn't believe in the afterlife so she hoped that death was a welcomed rest for them. They explored until the sun got low in the sky.

"Guys we should go inside and set up now." Matt said, turning to the house. They picked up the equipment from the ground outside and walked up the creaking steps to the front door. Lila pulled out a small camera and filmed Sara as she turned the doorknob and pushed. The door gave way with a small squeak. They slowly made their way inside. The entry way was covered in dust but other than that, it looked as though the owners had just stepped out for a moment. There was furniture set up as if company was expected. The long dining room table was set as though the sorority girls were going to sit down to dinner together. They made their way down the hall and through each room. Colin and Lila were shooting footage of everything. Finally they made their way to the living room. It was beautifully decorated and the fireplace even had logs in it ready to be lit.

"Matt and I will set up the cameras in the rooms and upstairs. Lila, you and Colin make sure that the feeds are working and tell us about positioning." Andrew ordered. He was excited. While the rest were busy with their tasks. Sara decided to watch the footage they had gotten before including her intro. She sat on the dusty old sofa and turned on the camera. The footage was even better than she had hoped and for a moment, she was extremely grateful that she had found such talent in Lila. As the video wrapped up she saw the frame of the entire house. Once more she took in the beauty until she noticed something. She paused the video and zoomed in. Up on the second floor in one of the bedroom windows stood a woman in a very old dress staring directly into the camera.

Sara took in a huge gasp of air and blinked. She looked again and the figure remained. She waved her hand toward Lila.

"What is it Sara?" She asked seeing Sara's horrified face.

"Colin, can you see me? How is this?" They heard from the microphone attached to the camera that Andrew was placing.

Lila moved over and looked at what Sara was pointing at. They replayed that part of the video and they were both speechless. They continued to watch through to the end and that was when they saw something even more startling. As Sara had approached the porch and was explaining Mary's hanging, the woman disappeared from the window and suddenly appeared right behind Sara holding a noose. They both gasped in fear.

"That's good Andrew, I think that's the best shot." Colin said into the walkie talkie.

Sara and Lila looked up to see the screen that Colin was watching. The video feed was of Andrew in the same room that the woman had been in in the video. "Andrew!" They both shrieked. Colin jumped in surprise.

"What?!" Andrew said from right behind them. They jumped and turned to him.

"How... you were just..." Sara stuttered.

"There is a 30 second delay. Geez what's wrong with you two?" He asked. They showed him the video while Colin helped Matt navigate setting up a camera in another room on the second story.

Andrew was just as stunned as they were. "I was just in there and there was nothing weird..." He said trying to talk himself down.

Then Lila got an idea. "Colin play back the footage you have of Andrew setting up the camera." She said.

"What..? Why?" He asked confused. He had been too distracted to hear their conversation.

"Just do it." Sara screeched. He did and they saw the room in night vision. It glowed in a soft green and they saw Andrew fumbling with the equipment.

"How long have you been doing this for now Andrew?" Colin teased but no one laughed.

Then just as Andrew leaned over to place the camera and backed away they saw her. The woman was right behind him holding a noose. Colin, who hadn't heard anything before that jumped back and screamed. "What the F***?!" They watched Andrew leave the room and the woman with the noose remained staring into the camera, unmoving. Then finally she turned her head and seemed to float out of the room.

They sat watching the camera in silence until the walkie talkie beeped, startling all of them.

"Colin, Colin! Is this ok? I don't want to be up here alone any longer. It gives me the creeps!" Matt said.

Colin immediately switched the video feed to Matt's camera only to see a close up of his face.

Sara held her breath. She wondered if the woman would appear in that room too. She grabbed the walkie talkie.

"Matt... uh... can you back up so we can see the room." She said with her voice shaking. They watched for 30 seconds and then saw him nod at the camera and back away. Just as they got a glimpse of the room, the feed cut and they heard a thud.

"Matt!" Sara screamed. They watched the screen and saw that it was flashing between black and night vison. When it stopped flashing, it showed something that drained Sara's blood. It was the woman holding the noose and standing next to a tall man in the same period clothing. And at the bottom of the screen they could see Matt's still body.

Andrew and Colin jumped up and ran to the staircase. Lila and Sara could hear their heavy footsteps above them. Lila stared at the screen with a strange expression on her face.

"Wait... that man... I've... I've seen him before. She reached for her laptop and opened it to a bookmarked page. It was an article from a newspaper covering the massacre of the sorority sisters. There were pictures of all 24 victims and a picture of the man who killed them. It was the same man.

Sara and Lila looked at both images in utter confusion. Then the feed from the room was cut completely and just as suddenly, the power went out. The darkness surrounded them and they screamed. In the corner of the room, a giant clock struck the hour. It was only 10 pm but it felt so much later. After the last chime, the power came back on and everything was quiet. Lila and Sara first checked to make sure the other was ok then looked around them. But when they looked at the walls, both felt as though the wind had been knocked out of them. All of the paintings, pictures and decorations were upside down.

They bolted up and ran to the stairway. As they climbed they saw the upside down portraits smiling sadistically at them. That's when Lila first saw it. Blood splatter on the wall. It looked fresh.

"Andrew! Colin! Matt!!??" She screamed and they ran up the stairs.

"Down here." Andrew's calm voice beckoned them to the last room on the right. Matt was sitting on the floor and Andrew was standing next to him. Colin was fiddling with the camera.

"I just told him what we saw." Andrew explained. "He doesn't believe me." Matt was clutching his head.

"What happened? Did they get you?" Sara asked breathlessly.

"Not you too... listen guys this isn't funny ok? My head hurts from knocking it on that shelf and I am not in the mood for a practical joke." Sara was about to try to reassure him that it was no joke when they heard the door behind them creak.

They turned to see a beautiful blond girl standing in the doorway. Her hair was disheveled and there was blood dripping from the side of her mouth and oozing from her sides and arms. "He's coming. You'd better run... although it never helped any of us." She said as her cold blue eyes looked past them to the window.

Then the lights went out again and flashed back on. She was gone and all that remained was a bloody hand print on the door frame.

"Believe me now?" Andrew said. Sara had no idea how he could care about that at a time like this.

"We need to leave." Sara said rushing to the door. But as she ran into the hall, she saw the same man as before wearing modern clothes and wielding a large knife. She saw blood splatter l lining the walls. He was blocking their way to the stairs. She looked around at the other bedroom doors that were slightly ajar. None of them would protect them. Then she looked up. There was a rope that pulled down a ladder to the attic.

"You guys!" She said as she yanked it. The man at the end of the hall started walking slowly towards her, undeterred by her possible escape. They all scrambled up the ladder and slammed the entry way shut before the man with the knife could reach them. They heard nothing. They sat in the dusty attic and silently tried to think of how to escape from the top floor of a mansion without going back into it. Though they were not really safer than before, the attic gave them a false sense of security and they all tried to breathe. Lila looked over at a box near them. She pulled out a very old painting. Though it was dark, she could make out that it was a couple. She pulled out her phone and used the light to look at the image. When she saw it clearly, she nearly dropped it.

It was the same man and woman they had seen in the video. But not only that, the man was identical to the mass murderer who killed the sorority girls 15 years prior. She read the bottom of the frame, "Mr. and Mrs. Lynch".

"Guys..." She said and showed the picture to the others.

"So what was this guy reincarnated or whatever?" Andrew asked. It was strange to hear that from a skeptic.

Just then, the ladder to the attic began to shake. They all looked around to find a way out. There was a tiny window at the other end of the attic. They ran over and Colin broke the old glass with his foot. Sara slid out first and they lowered her on to a part of the roof over the second story. Then it was Lila's turn. When they were both out, they crawled along the shingles to find a place they could climb down to the ground. They found nothing. By time the guys had slipped out, they had found the only possible way off the roof was to lower down into one of the bedroom windows. Andrew went first to break the window and help grab the others. Lila went first, then Colin. When it was Sara's turn she briefly looked around the property and the dirt road. The moon was much brighter than she thought it was and it lit the whole plantation. That was how she saw him. There standing against an old truck was a man, just watching the house and watching them climbing in. He didn't move.

"Do you see that man?" She asked Matt. He looked to where she was pointing and shivered. Something about the man by the truck gave him a sickening feeling.

"Yea... but we can't worry about him right now. We have to get out of here." Matt said.

He helped her lower down then quickly climbed down himself. They all made their way to the door and into the hall. Just as soon as they had stepped into the hall, the man reappeared with his bloody knife.

"Into the rooms!" Andrew screamed and they split up into each room.

They slammed the doors and turned the latches, each praying that the doors would hold from the phantom killer. But no sooner had they each locked the doors when a chorus of screams sounded. Hearing this, Sara turned around to face the room she was in. There was blood everywhere. The walls were covered and there on the bed was the body of a dead girl who had been stabbed over 10 times. Sara let out a cry. She heard the same sound come from Lila in the room next to her. They were all seeing the crime scenes of the girl that had died in each room.

Tears rolled down Sara's face. She ran to the window to try to open it. She would jump if she had to. A broken leg was better than dying. But it wouldn't budge.

"It won't open. They are nailed shut from the outside. He was very clever." A voice said from behind her. Sara turned to see the dead girl sitting up on her bed, the blood still dripping out of her wounds. He lifeless eyes seemed to look right through Sara. Sara screamed and rammed herself against the window. She would break the glass if she had to.

"You'll never make it. He planned this too well. The others that live here are loyal to him. They will help him to kill you. Just like they did for us." The dead girl said. Blood sprayed out of her mouth as she spoke but she didn't seem to notice. Sara tried not to look at her but felt a pulling sensation and her eyes were drawn back to the blood soaked girl on the bed. As soon as she made eye contact the lights went out again then flashed back on. The room was clean and the girl was gone. Then the door swung open. But the hall was empty. Sara poked her head out just enough to see her crew doing the same. They bolted towards the stairs only to see 24 bloody girls standing at the bottom staring up at them.

"He likes the chase. He likes the chase." They all chanted in a haunting harmony. Then they began climbing the stairs. They turned back to the hallway to see the man with the blade and the woman with the noose.

They moved towards them, slowly at first but then began to speed up, disappearing and reappearing closer and closer. Colin panicked and ran into the closest bedroom and slammed the door. Sara could him them trying to break the window. The woman with the noose smiled as she walked right through the door. There was a crashing sound then a thud. Then the door swung open slowly. Lila ran in to see if Colin had made it but as soon as she peered out the window she let out a horrible scream. She saw Colin swinging below from a noose. She turned back to look at her friends in horror but the door slammed shut once more and both phantoms were gone.

Seconds later there were terrible screams and then a gurgling sound. And once more the door swung open slowly. Lila was on the bed covered in her own blood with stab marks all over her body. Her eyes were looking up to the ceiling as if looking a God.

Sara almost ran into her but Matt grabbed her. He turned to look at the mob of dead sorority girls who stood staring with vacant expressions repeating, "He likes the chase."

"Help us!" He screamed. They ignored him. He grabbed Sara's arm and pulled her into the crowd.

"They aren't going to hurt us. They are his victims." He said and he and Sara ran down the stairs. Andrew couldn't move, he was frozen in fear. Andrew had never believed in the supernatural and couldn't process it. Matt and Sara ran to the front door and flung it open. Sara was about to yell for Andrew but at that very moment they saw a body drop from above the porch and swing in the same spot that Mary Lynch and Gary Lindale had hung themselves year before.

"Andrew!!!" Sara screamed. Matt dragged her to the car and fumbled with the keys. Finally he opened the doors and they both got inside and locked the doors. Sara looked at the house, now able to see it clearly in the moonlight. She saw Andrew's and Colin's bodies hanging from their nooses and looked up to the bedroom where Lila had been murdered. In the window stood the man with the knife. Next to him, stood a lifeless Lila. In all of the other windows, the Sorority sisters stood looking out into the night with their dead stares. Matt revved the engine and turned the van sharply to get back on the dirt road. That's when they saw the man with the truck. He stared at them. His gaze was unwavering. After a few moments he got in his truck and turned on his bright lights. Then he revved his engine and slammed on the accelerator. He was driving right at them.

"What the F*** is he doing?" Matt asked in shock. He didn't have time or room to get out of the way and Sara braced herself for the impact. But as soon as the truck would have touched the front fender, it disappeared. Matt looked around and in the rear view mirror. There was no sign of it.

"Just go!" Sara yelled.

And they did. They drove to the police station and told them everything that had happened. The police refused to go to the house until the morning and Matt and Sara stayed in their cell the rest of the night.

In the morning they all went back. It was just as they had left it. The police did their reports and the coroner was called. When they had gotten all their equipment out, Sara asked if they could leave. One of the cops agreed to take them back to their hotel and they climbed in the back of a car. Sara let her look once more at the big house. She looked up at the room where Lila had died. There in the window was Lila looking back at her. She waved a sad goodbye and disappeared.

Sara was institutionalized a week later and this is the only story she will ever tell.